"YOU PLAY TERRIBLY," A VOICE ANNOUNCED.

Madeline jumped at the sound and whirled around. A tall man stood in the doorway, smiling. "What are you doing here?" she demanded.

"I . . . live here." He drew himself up into that disapproving stance she remembered so well from the day he had walked her home from Watier's.

"You live here?" she repeated in confusion.

"I am Frederick's tutor." He crossed his arms across his chest and looked defiant.

"Oh. I am Frederick's cousin. My name is Madeline Delaney, in case you do not recall." She raised a brow at him and dared him to comment. He merely regarded her with some interest. "As you doubtless have guessed, I am here to learn the error of my reckless ways, so you needn't launch into another of your lectures on propriety."

"Please forgive my insufferability on that occasion. I was not in the best of tempers, for unrelated reasons, that day. I am Devin Forth, in case *you* do not recall. I am charmed to make your acquaintance." He shook her hand solemnly, but his gray-green eyes had a suspicious gleam. Madeline thought she had heard him murmur, "Mad Maddie," under his breath, but that was impossible.

BOOK YOUR PLACE ON OUR WEBSITE AND MAKE THE READING CONNECTION!

We've created a customized website just for our very special readers, where you can get the inside scoop on everything that's going on with Zebra, Pinnacle and Kensington books.

When you come online, you'll have the exciting opportunity to:

- View covers of upcoming books
- Read sample chapters
- Learn about our future publishing schedule (listed by publication month *and author*)
- Find out when your favorite authors will be visiting a city near you
- Search for and order backlist books from our online catalog
- Check out author bios and background information
- Send e-mail to your favorite authors
- Meet the Kensington staff online
- Join us in weekly chats with authors, readers and other guests
- Get writing guidelines
- AND MUCH MORE!

**Visit our website at
http://www.zebrabooks.com**

THE SCANDALOUS MISS DELANEY

Catherine Blair

Zebra Books
Kensington Publishing Corp.
http://www.zebrabooks.com

For Selina Noramly,
with all my gratitude.

ZEBRA BOOKS are published by

Kensington Publishing Corp.
850 Third Avenue
New York, NY 10022

Copyright © 1999 by Noelle Gracy

First Printing: August, 1999
10 9 8 7 6 5 4 3 2 1

Printed in the United States of America

One

"Ruined!"

Madeline cringed at the word, but resisted the temptation to hide her face in an embroidered sofa cushion and lapse into hysterics. She forced her chin up and pretended that this was an ordinary scold for a typical prank.

"I never thought I would see the day when my daughter should shame me so!" her father continued.

She watched the veins in his forehead swell and shrank farther back onto the sofa.

"Your mother, rest her soul, was a lady and not some fast hussy! I put your hoydenish conduct down to girlish high spirits until now, but I never thought you would be so ill bred as to ruin yourself."

This was a good deal worse than she had expected. He was pacing the room, picking up and putting down objects as though he were considering which to throw.

"Papa, I will not be ruined!" she pleaded.

"You most certainly are. You are the daughter

of a peer. You were educated in the manners of society. How could you throw it away in a moment by dancing the waltz before you were given permission at Almack's? Not to mention doing so with a man who is on the very fringe of gentility. He is not the kind of man any hostess should have in her drawing room! And besides dancing with this . . . person, this well-known rake, you were seen immediately after the dance to leave the room with him to walk unchaperoned in the garden!"

Madeline tried to listen to him, but she was so tired. What had begun as a kind of fantasy, full of excitement and romance, was now a nightmare. It was well past four o'clock in the morning, and her father was ranting, red-faced and ludicrous, in his nightshirt and bare feet. Her duenna sat in the corner producing a constant, keening wail consisting mainly of bewildered requests that the Almighty explain what she had done to deserve this. Her own dress was crumpled, her slippers were ruined, and all the curl in her hair had turned to frizzles.

"But everyone dances the waltz these days," she protested. "People will forget by tomorrow night. It will be a nine-day wonder at the most."

"When Mrs. Benjamin found you, he was . . . he was . . . embracing you! You were seen by several people, and will be the talk of the town by tomorrow morning!" His voice rose to such a fevered pitch that his daughter began to worry seriously for his health.

"I didn't enjoy it," she replied in a small voice, forgetting in her anguish all strictures of posture and curling her feet up on the cushions so that she could clasp her hands around her knees.

This pronouncement was obviously no consolation. Lord Albert Delaney gave a roar like a bull. "You cannot tell me that you did not know this was wrong! Did I raise you to be a trollop?"

Mrs. Benjamin gave an affronted gasp.

"And him!" Lord Delaney spat out. "He certainly should have known better. Walking in the garden, indeed. Embracing!" He said this word with the greatest distaste. "Even if you haven't two brains to rub together, he should never have allowed you to compromise your reputation in such a manner. I should call that cad out!"

"Papa!"

"Do take your dirty slippers off the upholstery, pet," Mrs. Benjamin requested, midwail.

"You will not call anyone out," Madeline said impatiently. "I am certain that Lord Lambrook will offer for me, and I shall marry him. Then the whole scandal shall be passed over." She had not actually thought about this possibility until the words were out of her mouth, and the idea of it rather shocked her. She certainly had not intended to get herself engaged only a few weeks into the season to a man she did not know.

"Lambrook!" The forehead vein reappeared. "That man would have been killed long ago if he had any honor! I know for a fact that he was called out at least twice and fled to the continent last year rather than face up to a duel. There are hundreds of rumors about him which are far from fit for the likes of you to hear. He is an unprincipled scoundrel, and I would never consider his suit. That man as a son-in-law!" He slammed his hand on his desk. "It is unthinkable! Furthermore—" he waggled a finger at his daughter—"I shudder to imagine how in debt the man is. We should have the house overrun with debt collectors the moment your engagement was announced. The River Tick, indeed. . . ." His voice trailed off, and he stood for a moment with his mouth a tight line.

"You have landed in it this time, Madeline," he said at last with a sigh. "I do not see a way out of it. If he were to make you an offer. . . ."

"He will. I will accept, and there will be no scandal. You will see." Madeline nodded vehemently.

"We shall see," her father conceded wearily. He briefly smoothed her dark gold hair in a distracted, but fond gesture. "You are not to leave the house until Lambrook has made his offer. I cannot believe that you would behave in such a madcap manner." He sighed and glanced at his daughter's duenna. That woman's face puckered in preparation.

"No more of that noise, I beg you!" Lord Delaney held up his hand in a preemptive gesture, "Mrs. Benjamin, it is not your fault that I have such a hoyden for a daughter. I would have employed a whole fleet of chaperons if I had known what a trouble this one child of mine would be. Take her to her room."

Without even leaving the house, Madeline knew that within two days she was the subject of the latest *on dit*. The doorbell was shockingly silent and the daily sheaf of mail agonizingly thin.

"On dit," she murmured to herself, testing the way it felt to say the word. She stared blankly across her small sitting room into the empty fire grate. She had always supposed it would be a little interesting to be the subject of a scandal. Notorious people were inevitably far more fascinating than those who gossiped about them. However, after several days of solitude, she was beginning to feel as though being the key character in the latest gossip was not quite the experience she thought it would be.

Then, of course, there was the matter of Lambrook not calling.

She had had a good deal of time over the two days to invent extremely exotic reasons to excuse his continued absence. She had established through Isabella, the one faithful friend who continued to communicate with her, that he had not been ill, in jail, killed, forced to flee to the continent, or in any such acceptable circumstances.

It was not as though she loved the man. She had only just been formally introduced to him the night of the incident! However, it was beyond insulting that he would simply not call. That he would not make any excuse for his behavior at all.

She looked down at the crumpled paper in her hand. Isabella had written a missive that morning, explaining the entire matter in the most unsatisfactory manner imaginable. She sat for another moment with an abstracted expression, twisting and retwisting the letter in her hands before sitting down to write a reply.

Dearest Isabella,

I thank you for sending me news of Lord Lambrook, though, as you know, it was hardly what I wished to hear. At first I did not believe that it could be true. Roderick seen at the opera with Lord Dancy's mistress? I did not know he was acquainted with her. But then, I realize now that I do not know him at all. Still, I deluded myself that you must have been mistaken.

But three whole days have passed, and he has not appeared. I fear for the worst, my dearest friend! I should have listened to your warning! I am an abandoned, ruined woman! Mrs. Benjamin has begun to rumble ominously about a trip to the country until the scandal blows over. But never fear, Bella, I have begun to formulate a plan.

She signed the note with a flourish and, feeling much improved, gave it to a footman to deliver.

She walked thoughtfully back to her room, then sat staring at the rose-striped wallpaper for a long time. Slowly, a pleased smile crossed her face.

Leaping to her feet, she raced to the clothespress in her dressing room and pulled out the heavy black cloak she had found the day before. It had been the inspiration for the plan. The plan that would set everything right.

Upon inspection, the cloak turned out to be much too warm to wear on a spring day, but it would have to do. She tried on a deep poke bonnet that satisfactorily covered her hair, but decided it did not hide her face enough. In its place she wore a yellow hat that had once belonged to a riding habit. It was too bright, but at least its veil somewhat obscured her features. The overall effect of the costume was somewhat ridiculous, especially with the long, brown ostrich feathers that curled rakishly over one ear, but there was nothing that could be done about it.

Poking her head out first to see if anyone was about, she crept down the hallway toward the servants' stairs. She could hear two of the chambermaids chattering as they tidied one of the rooms, but no one noticed as she slipped down the back stairs and into the mews at the rear of the house. The sky was oppressively heavy with clouds. She considered going back for an umbrella, but decided she did not have the time to go back and must take her chances with the weather.

Now, to find Lambrook. In order to obtain his address, she had decided to ask at a shop he might frequent. She felt this was particularly clever, in that she would not have to speak to anyone who might know her. Any shop owner would

be unlikely to recognize her in the future. It was
not far to St. James Street, but walking might
mean that she would run into someone she knew.
She checked the amount of money in her reticule.
It was not very much, and she realized that she
had no idea of what a cabfare would be. She had
nearly always been out in the family carriages, and
on the few occasions she had been in a hackney,
Mrs. Benjamin had taken care of the payment.

Perhaps Lambrook lived quite far away. She had
best save her money in case the trip there was
expensive. Resolved, she darted as best she could
along side streets, thankful that she did not have
a great distance to go. Her strange garb occa-
sioned stares from passersby, but luckily it was not
yet the fashionable hour for promenading.

She entered the shop of a popular tobacconist,
and was almost overpowered by the rich, heavy
smell of tobacco. Inside, it was dim and crowded
with what seemed to be hundreds and hundreds
of jars. She did not afford herself the luxury of
looking about her more closely, but kept her head
ducked down, hoping that the darkness of the
shop's interior and the veil of her hat would be
enough to obscure her face from recognition. The
tobacconist scrutinized her with some suspicion
when she asked if Lord Lambrook numbered
amongst his customers.

"It's just that . . . I want to buy a present for
him . . . some tobacco . . . and I don't know
where to have it sent," she prevaricated quickly.
The shop owner's jaw became even more set at

the notion of a young lady sending gifts to a man of such dubious reputation as Lambrook. "He's my cousin," she added in desperation. "It is his birthday," she tacked on for good measure. Finally the man unbent and allowed her to purchase some rather exorbitantly expensive snuff and pretended not to notice as she looked at the address he had it sent to.

"Who shall I say it's from, miss?" he asked, disapproval terribly apparent on his face.

"What? Oh! I . . . that is . . . his cousin . . . Cousin Hattie." She attempted a weak smile that the tobacconist did not reciprocate.

Escaping from the shop, she hired a hansom cab. The inside smelled strongly of ale, and the straw on the floor looked as though it might harbor a multitude of unpleasant surprises. She tried to keep her feet from touching it.

Unlike the tobacconist, if the driver had any misgivings as to conveying a strangely garbed female alone to the private residence of a well-known gentleman, he gave no indication. As she approached the house, she herself began to feel slight qualms. Up to now, she had been so intent on carrying out her plan to get there that she had not given any real thought as to what she would do once she was actually at his house. Certainly it was not acceptable for single young ladies to go calling alone upon notorious gentlemen. It only added to her discomfort to note that the house was in a part of town that was not at all fashionable, and that it looked to be in a state of some shabbiness.

Her heart pounding, she knocked on the door. There was no response for such a long time that she had nearly made up her mind to abandon the plan and slink home. At last the door was opened by a very large, square-jawed butler who gazed impassively at her cloak and veil as if this were the very thing he had expected.

"I would like to see Lord Lambrook," she faltered.

"His Grace is not at home," was the immediate, repressive reply. Although Madeline's plans were vague, they definitely included speaking in person with Lord Lambrook.

"Where could I find him?" she asked desperately, knowing that "not at home" often meant not wanting to see anyone. "It is very important that I talk to him."

"I believe my lord might be found at his club—Watier's," the butler volunteered unexpectedly.

She swore to herself, including an epithet she had just learned from the hansom driver. That meant another cab fare. Would they even let her in the door at Watier's? Could they send someone in to get him for her? She saw the tobacconist's boy, who had watched her with interest in the shop, leap off a dray at the end of the street. So, hastily thanking the butler, she again hailed a hansom and directed the driver to go toward Pall Mall.

As the morning had dragged on with nothing

but frustrating results, she began to regret the impunity of her actions. The cloak was becoming unbearably hot and kept getting tangled about her. The constant presence of spots on the lace of the veil before her eyes had given her a headache. Perhaps Lord Lambrook would be angry when he saw her. Perhaps he had left Watier's and was even now calling on her at her home. Yes, it was almost certain that he was. Perhaps at this very moment her father was sending someone up to find her. Thankfully, the ride was not a long one, and she got out in front of the club before she had convinced herself to tell the driver to take her home.

She stood outside the entrance of the gentlemen's club for a few moments, unsure of what course of action to take. After some mental debate, she resolved to ask someone going into the club to retrieve Lord Lambrook for her. The first man to enter, she recognized as someone she had been introduced to at some point, so she quickly withdrew and looked away with the hopes that he would not notice her. It was difficult to imagine how he could not notice a woman whose dress made her resemble a canary in mourning. After some time, a stranger approached the door, and she accosted him with her request.

He looked at her in some confusion, assessing the likelihood that she had escaped from Bedlam. "I am sorry, madam," he muttered at last and attempted to go.

"But, sir, you do not understand! It is an emergency. You must help me." Madeline clung dramatically to his sleeve. She could barely see him through the veil of the hat, but he looked as though he might be vacillating.

"But I do not belong to Watier's," he protested, his straight, dark brows drawing together over rather pleasing gray-green eyes.

"Please, sir! It is a long and complex story. I am in a terrible scrape, and I desperately need your help. Simply go in and ask for him. I know that he will come out. You know they will not let me in." At this point, as an added insult to her already frayed patience, single, fat raindrops began to splatter on the pavement at irregular intervals.

The stranger looked more annoyed than sympathetic. He shook her arm off impatiently, and then, unexpectedly, he sighed and entered the club.

Madeline waited for what seemed like an interminable age, which only added to her growing nervousness. She tried to use this time to prepare a speech that would express her reason for coming, but the words in her mind were all ajumble. At last the door opened and her rescuer reappeared, accompanied by Lord Lambrook. The contrast between the two men was quite marked. The stranger stood stiff with disapproval while Lambrook visibly drooped. His arm was flung around the stranger's shoulders in a familiar manner which the other man obviously found odious. They were both dark-haired and well built, but the stranger looked tidy, although his clothes were not in the first stare of fashion. Lambrook, in contrast, seemed positively dissipated. He wore evening clothes in the middle of the day. Though fashionable, they were rumpled and stained, and his cravat was entirely undone. Somehow he was not quite so dashing as she recalled.

"What the devil do you want?" he demanded thickly.

"Oh, Lord Lambrook, you've come! It is me, Madeline." She drew back the veil of the hat and peered into his face. He smelled distinctly of drink, despite the fact that it was only two o'clock in the afternoon.

"Who?" He squinted at her confusedly. "It is too damned bright out here."

"Madeline Delaney. I . . . You . . . You . . . we met the night before last at Lady Mcalington-Smythe's ball. The garden?" She felt foolish having to prompt him so. Although she kept her eyes averted from the man Lambrook leaned so heavily upon, she felt the disdain positively radiate from him.

"Oh, yes," Lambrook said at last, a slow smile creeping across his handsome but somewhat bestubbled face, "The little girl from the ball. . . ." He seemed to reminisce for a moment. "Well, what of it?"

"What of it?!" Madeline heard her voice go shrill. "My father waits for you to call on me!"

Lord Lambrook looked at her blankly for a moment and then burst into loud, uninhibited laughter. Madeline was stricken. "You do not intend to offer for me?"

"Why would I?"

"I am ruined!" This interview was, indeed, going badly. The stranger shifted uncomfortably and valiantly appeared not to have heard.

"You are a little fool," Lambrook responded with an exaggerated dismissive gesture. "A meaningless flirtation. It is not as though you are with child or any such thing." He did not seem to notice that she blanched at this. "Not that I suppose it would matter if you were. Your father is an old man and a petty little baron. He would never call out someone of my social standing. Now I will thank you to leave and not bother me over this matter again. Good day, Miss Melanie." He sketched a slight bow, turned on his heel, and left her there on the street.

For a long moment, Madeline stood on the sidewalk, her heart not beating. This could not possibly be happening.

"Shall I call you a cab?" The stranger's words brought her back to reality.

"I . . . no thank you." She was not willing to admit that after the unexpected expenditure of the snuff, she did not have enough money to hire a hansom. "I shall walk." She tugged the veil back into place to hide the tears that stung her eyes. Starting down the street, she was surprised to find the stranger had fallen into step beside her. The rain had begun to fall in earnest now, and he opened his umbrella over them both. His scowl indicated that he was performing a duty, not charity.

"You needn't come with me," she said in an irritated tone.

"I will walk you home," he replied tersely. "I hope it is not far."

"No, not far at all. I suppose I could have taken a hansom, but it is really much too close for that." For the first time, she was aware that he was much younger than she had previously thought. Probably only in his early thirties. It was his impatient expression that made him look older.

"I doubt you could have found an empty one in this weather." The streets were indeed clogged with carriages, and every hansom seemed to have an occupant. He began walking very quickly in the direction she indicated.

"I am so sorry to have involved you in this imbroglio," she began after a few moments, a little breathless from trotting to keep up with him. "I am not always like this, really." She very nearly had to shout at him over the drumming of the rain on the umbrella.

His frown did not clear. "I am in a hurry." He held out his arm to her ungraciously as she leapt over an overflowing curb. Madeline noted with a surge of guilt that his left shoulder was getting wet, since he held the umbrella mostly over her. His shoulders were very broad, but his coat had the unfortunate shininess of worn, cheap fabric. He seemed to be dressed in mourning. Perhaps that accounted for his irritability.

"I would never usually go out on my own."

He made a small noise in his throat that indicated his disbelief.

"You will not mention this incident, of course." She was beginning to grow weary of walking so fast, and the cloak seemed to be getting heavier as its hem dragged through puddles.

"No." He did not even look at her.

"This whole incident did not turn out at all as I had intended," she continued desperately.

The man stopped, and Madeline nearly walked out from under the cover of the umbrella. "Miss," he snapped, "I find that people like you always have the best intentions and the worst results."

"People like me?" Madeline looked up at him, appalled. "How do you know anything about me? How was I to know Lambrook was a man like that?"

"I am certain that you were told and that you simply did not choose to listen." He adopted a lecturing tone, "You would have done better to heed your parents; then you would not be in this . . . situation. The trouble with young women today is that they have a good deal too much freedom and no sense at all. I am sure you thought that man was dashing. You most likely fancied yourself quite daring to be associating with a man of his ilk and off traipsing about the town without even a maid to look after you. If my sisters showed any symptoms of such immodest behavior, I should lock them up."

He scowled into the rain for a moment. "That man should be shot." He spat out the words in disgust. Some of his loathing seemed to apply to herself as well. She was not the kind of woman with whom a stuffy, upstanding man such as himself would want to associate.

They walked the rest of the way in silence. Madeline felt a resentment from him that seemed out of proportion to the inconvenience she was causing him. At this point, she was too humiliated to care. "There is my house," she said at last, gesturing toward where it stood at one side of the square. Her companion looked at it and snorted in derision. She held her head high, striving at the last moment for a little dignity. "Thank you very much Mr. . . ."

"Forth," he replied reluctantly.

"I am Madeline Delaney. I hope you will understand if I do not invite you in for tea. My father is unaware that I have gone out."

"Of course he is," was the dry reply. Madeline regarded him for a moment with compressed lips and leveled brows, then dipped a low curtsy and ran lightly toward the mews entrance.

Devin Forth watched her go, resisting the urge to run after her and apologize. He was not usually so full of barbed replies and vituperative comments. After all, she was just some silly chit who, like countless others before her, had fallen in love with a man who used her. She was not his responsibility. He had done his duty by walking her home. It was not his fault that she had gone and ruined herself. She should not have gone haring off on her own to try to meet the man who obviously had no further use for her. It was a sad story, really.

But it was not his sad story. He had problems of his own. The meeting with his father's solicitor had not been at all pleasant. He had known for years that his family fortunes had been sliding, but he had had no idea how much his father had hidden from them while still alive. He thought of Anne and Margaret, and his hand unconsciously reached for the letter in his waistcoat pocket. It seemed there was no other choice.

Two

"Madeline!" Mrs. Benjamin's voice rose shrilly up the stairway. Her charge only had time to pull off the veiled hat and to change her direction, so that it appeared she was coming downstairs from the third floor rather than across the hallway from the servant's stairs, before her duenna appeared. "Where have you been?" the woman asked with a frown.

"I . . . I was in the attic looking through some old trunks." Madeline tried to look sulky and disinterested rather than guilty. "I found this old cloak. Don't you think it would make a nice . . . costume?" She removed the garment immediately, hoping that Mrs. Benjamin would not notice that it was soaked.

"If you wanted to look like a highwayman, perhaps," the older woman replied tartly. "Now, don't go disappearing again. Laws, the house is in such a jumble. Your father has decided that you shall remove to the country tomorrow morning. I don't know what the man is thinking to expect me to be able to get your things together that fast."

"What?" Madeline tried not to look too delighted. "The country?"

"I know you are upset my dear, but you must understand. Your father does not feel that he could countenance a match between you and Lord Lambrook even if Lambrook did offer. Which he has not." Mrs. Benjamin managed to look both reproving and sympathetic at the same time. "And I think he is right not to do so. He is not the kind of man who would make you a good husband. I know they say rakes make the best husbands, but I never felt you could depend too much on a man's reforming once he was married. Mr. Benjamin, well, he himself— But that is another story. You will find in a few weeks that you will never think about Lord Lambrook at all. Really, pet, he is not the kind of man I would wish you to marry. I have heard a little about him since the . . . the Incident, and we may count ourselves quite lucky that he has not proposed. I shudder to think if your father had accepted. . . ."

She clicked her tongue against her teeth and shook her head. "Well, you may like the country more than you think you will," she continued, coaxingly. "It will be quite pleasant to have a little rest. Besides, your uncle Edmund and aunt Enid in Somerset will be delighted to have you spend some time with them. You haven't seen your cousin for years. He must be nine or ten by now."

She herded the girl back to her rooms and began to fuss with the packing. Madeline felt weak with relief that her companion was too distracted to notice her strange clothing and behavior. She balled up the cloak and shoved it and the much-damaged yellow hat to the back of the clothes-press.

While Mrs. Benjamin made harried noises regarding the necessity of packing with so little notice, Madeline dashed off another note to Isabella telling her of her impending departure and begging to see her before she was forced to leave. She handed the missive to a footman and gave him instructions, then steeled herself for a meeting with her father.

"Papa," she called softly as she pushed open the door of his study.

"Ah, I see that Mrs. Benjamin has found you. Come in."

Madeline schooled her features to express contrition rather than the chaos of humiliation, anger, frustration, and relief that was swirling inside her. Her father was sitting at his desk, barely visible behind stacks of books and papers. He stood immediately when she entered and indicated that she should seat herself in one of the seats by the fire he kept burning in the hearth all year round. This was apparently not going to be a short interview. Lord Albert removed a large stack of books from his desk to create a gap through which he could observe her.

"Lambrook has not asked for your hand," he

began, looking extremely forbidding behind his ramparts.

"I know, Papa," she replied humbly, wishing she had not been so foolish as to have announced to him that a proposal was ever a possibility.

"I suppose there are some who would call me a coward for not calling him out."

"No! There is no need for that, I assure you!"

"Regardless, rather than make a scandalous event even more so, I have decided to send you to your uncle's estate." He paused, and regarded her intently. "I must make it clear to you, however you feel about Lambrook, and whether he proposed or not, I could never countenance a match between you. He is a rake and a fortune hunter."

Madeline dropped her eyes to the carpet and nodded.

Her father seemed surprised at this lack of reaction. "I know how disappointed you are to miss the rest of the season," he pressed on, "but I cannot help but feel this is the best thing for your reputation and for you. You need to learn some sense, girl. I should have made you wait another year before your come out. You are perpetually in some scrape or another. If I had thought a daughter of mine—"

She interrupted before he could begin that litany again. "I know Papa. I think you are right."

"Ah . . . Well, I am glad you have come to your senses." He paused for a moment, bewildered that she had made no argument. "Then I suppose it is settled."

* * *

"Mr. Forth!" Devin heard the summons, but was tempted to pretend he had not. It was Frederick's mother, Lady Hesstrow. "Mr. Forth, although I know you are busy with your duties tutoring my son, I am having a dinner party tonight. Unfortunately, Mr. Garring had to cancel at the last moment due to illness. I know I can depend on you to make up the numbers. Please join us at eight o'clock. Dressed appropriately, of course." She smiled sweetly and waved her hand in dismissal.

Devin bowed his head with the minimum civility possible and exited before he could say anything regrettable. It was insulting to be used as a spare guest who could be trotted out to do the pretty when needed and shoved back into a cupboard when not. On the occasions when he was invited to dine with company, he was referred to as "our dear house guest" or "our dear cousin." The rest of the time he was only "the tutor." If he was referred to at all.

Lord Hesstrow had asked Devin to join him in riding a few times, and on occasion had made a kind of oblique apology for his wife's behavior. However, he was not really the kind of man who liked to involve himself in aspects of life other than hunting, shooting, and fishing, and so conveniently chose not to think of the matter at all. In fact, seeing Devin about the house appeared to make him feel guilty. He was always over-hearty in his greetings and talked a bit too loudly. In the past week, Devin had learned to avoid both Hesstrow and his wife as much as possible.

"You look very cross," Frederick commented as Forth entered the schoolroom.

Forcing his features into more neutral lines, Devin smoothed the boy's hair. "Forgive me, Freddie," he said good-naturedly. "I do not intend to be cross with you."

"More Horrible History today? Last time you were telling me that Mary went to Holland to marry her uncle William."

"He was her cousin. Royalty often marry their cousins." Devin moved to the front of the schoolroom and assumed a pose he had come to think of as tutorish.

Frederick looked horrified. "I would *not* like to marry my cousin. She is horribly rotten-awful. She was here the summer before last summer—no, the summer when I was seven—and she is the worst cousin in the world. She got scolded every day. She locked me in the linen closet, and I was really little then, so I was just the tiniest bit scared. It was a long time ago," he explained defensively.

Devin smiled understandingly.

"She is really ugly and has frizzy yellow hair. You would have to pay me a hundred thousand pounds to marry her."

"That is really no way to speak about a relation," Devin reminded him mildly.

"She was always having these ideas, and she would make me help her with her plans, and then I would always get into trouble." Frederick let out a worldly sigh. "Once she convinced me to run away—to be a shepherd—with her. I had to help her knot the sheets together, and we were going to climb out the window, but Maddie got stuck hanging out there because she got scared of the height, so a footman had to get a ladder and come rescue her."

Devin suppressed a smile. "A shepherd?"

"Well, it sounded like fun. I was little then," Frederick reminded him. "Madeline is in London now, doing her season. A London season is like grouse season only you are hunting for a husband instead of grouse. I hope someone else marries her or else I might have to."

"Even if she does not receive an offer, I very much doubt that you will be called upon to do so."

"I don't think anyone will offer," the boy said, a fist jammed despondently into his cheek. "Mama said she was getting a reputation for being fast. I know what fast means." He raised his eyebrows in a man-of-the-world fashion.

"Do you?" Devin knew he should insist that they return to the history of monarchs of England, but his curiosity got the upper hand.

"It means that she blinks like this"—Frederick fluttered his lashes—"very fast, and men think she is telling them she wants to get married. Nice men don't like girls who are fast at them."

"That is an interesting assessment," Devin commented dryly. "Now, I think we should get back to William and Mary."

"I wouldn't like girls who were fast at me," Frederick continued thoughtfully. "Of course, I don't like girls at all. I like dogs and horses."

"William and Mary," Devin announced sternly. They were about to start again when there was a scratch at the door and a maid entered.

"Lady Hesstrow wants Master Frederick cleaned up for guests and down in the drawing room this very minute," she explained.

Frederick looked dismayed. "Good clothes? I hate the good clothes. They itch."

Devin could not resist laughing. "Watch out, Frederick. It might be your cousin, come to be fast to you." He fluttered his lashes predatorially at Frederick, who howled in mock panic.

As the boy pounded out of the room and down the stairs, Devin ran a hand through his hair in a gesture that he had not realized had become habitual. This had been a terrible idea right from the start. It had seemed so sensible. He had not anticipated the constant humiliation of being the poor relation.

However, even with Lady Hesstrow's constant jabs regarding social station, he did not really regret the decision. His sisters depended on the money he sent them, and with it, they would never need to know personally the degradation of working as practically a servant. Margaret had often chided him, stating that it would have been much more sensible for them all to attempt to contract advantageous marriages.

As if he would ask her to do so when she was

obviously becoming quite fond of the curate. He sat down and stretched his long legs before him. But there was always himself. At the time of Margaret's suggestion, he had rejected that option in outraged indignation, stating that he would never dupe a young lady into marrying him just so her wealth could support his family. Even though he still felt that his current uncomfortable situation was preferable to living a life of obligation to some young miss's father, there were times when he envied men who had no qualms about taking this route out of debt.

His thoughts again coursed inexplicably back to the day when he had been in London to pay a less than satisfactory visit to his family's solicitor. Until then, he had not known how very far his father had dug the family into debt before having the bad grace to contract an inflammation of the lungs. It had been the day that had sealed his fate as a poor relation.

It was ironic that on the same day he had met the ridiculous girl in the laughable cloak and the yellow hat. He could not help smiling at the memory. It was a sad enough story, but the foolish creature had made a cake of herself by throwing herself at her former lover. Most likely fancy pieces and mistresses knew better how to gracefully accept the termination of a relationship than women of the upper ten thousand, he mused. Running a man to earth at his own club and causing a scene outside it, dressed like some outlandish actress was hardly acceptable behavior. Even if the man was obviously a complete rake. It would have been better to take his rejection with a modicum of dignity, but she was young and obviously of Quality. Judging from her house and its entirely genteel situation in Mayfair, she was probably in expectation of quite a healthy dowry. Until she had been ruined, that is.

He remembered the man named Lambrook, and his jaw set in anger. He should have landed that man a facer. If he had not been so distracted by the sudden clarification of his family's financial situation, he would have. She was little more than a child, and the man had taken advantage of her. Thoughtless and spoiled or not, no woman deserved what he had put her through. Devin got up and began to prowl the room impatiently. It did no good to pity her. He wasn't likely to ever see her again.

"Maddie!" Isabella held out her arms to her friend. "I came over the instant I heard. Are you really going away? I have not seen you in days! You must tell me exactly what has happened. The rumors are extremely confused and your letters have not been very clear at all, I'm afraid." Isabella was flushed with anxiety, but, annoyingly, that only made her look prettier. Somehow, with her dark hair and eyes, blushes did not mar her complexion. Madeline always felt that her own fair coloring could not support pink cheeks. Unfortunately, she had had much cause to blush of late.

"Bella, I am in the most dreadful coil. I don't know how it happened." She flopped onto the sofa despondently.

"However did you come to be involved with Lambrook? I had no idea you had been introduced."

"Do you remember how just the other day I was saying that I was bored of all the proper society types and wanted to meet interesting, scandalous people?"

Isabella sat down on a chair beside her friend and nodded apprehensively. "But Lord Lambrook! It is said that he keeps a mistress here—and in France, too—and that he has fathered several children out of wedlock! He is not received in the best of houses."

Madeline groaned. "Well, I didn't know he was that reprehensible, but I knew that he was not quite all that is proper. I was intrigued." She raised her brows in a helpless expression.

"So I contrived to be introduced to him in the most shameless way by racing up to the hostess and asking after her daughter!" She could not repress a gurgle of laughter at the memory. "Do you remember Maria Mealington-Smythe from Miss Patten's Academy? Well, I hardly knew her at all myself." Madeline sat up, her coif entirely disassembled. She impatiently pushed a fallen lock of hair from her face without noticing. "So, Maria's mama was obliged to introduce Lambrook to me, though she hardly looked as though she wanted to. Oh"—she pounded a pillow in a sudden fit of annoyance—"I should have known!"

"Do go on!" Isabella urged, entirely enraptured at this Cheltenham tragedy unfolding in the drawing room.

"So he was polite to me, even if he did look me up and down a bit, and I thought he was no worse than sorts like Lord Reginald Stedtson, who still insists on calling on me and proposing. Well, that is, he used to until this happened. Happily, Papa knew how I detested him and never accepted. How odious!" She leapt up and began to pace the room. "And he—Lambrook, I mean, is not old. I suppose he is even handsome. Not that I would think so now! I have heard that he never even speaks to young ladies in their first season—" she laughed ruefully— "and I thought perhaps I could pique his interest in me."

"Madeline!" Isabella exclaimed in agony.

"I flirted with him terribly, and—Oh! It is so embarrassing! He asked me to dance, and I said that I could not because it was a waltz." She threw her friend a look of contrition and continued her pacing.

"And you have not yet been given permission at Almack's. But I heard that you *did* waltz."

"I am getting to that. He said that I should not let convention stand in our way, and asked if I had any backbone and things like that."

"Oh, dear." Isabella knew her friend well.

"So we did waltz, and I thought it would be good sport, Lambrook being a bit dashing, but everyone stared so. It was highly unpleasant. I felt quite as though I were the lead actress in a play. Every quizzing glass in the room was trained on us. I suppose he is a good dancer, though," she added fairly.

"How can you say that!" Isabella cried.

"Oh, but it is worse." Madeline returned to the sofa. She sat down and lowered her voice. "After the dance he led me out into the garden, and no one was there, and he kissed me."

Isabella's gasp showed that this part of the story had not been made public. "What was it like?" she asked, horrified and fascinated.

Madeline wrinkled her nose. "Wet," she pronounced. "And our faces seemed to get in the way of each other." To her friend's shock, she began to laugh. "And his nose . . ." She was laughing so hard that she could hardly get the words out.

"His nose?"

"I could hear . . . his breath . . . whistling in and out," Madeline shrieked with glee and then demonstrated this effect.

"Maddie! Have you no sensibilities? You are ruined. You will never get a respectable offer of marriage!" Isabella's eyes went wide to emphasize the magnitude of this pronouncement. "And I was certain that Sir George Wycoff was on the point of making an offer."

"I know," Madeline replied with a lopsided smile and a shrug meant to convince her friend that she did not care.

"But Sir George is such a very good catch." Isabella suddenly conceived a deep interest in the pattern of the carpet. "And he is such a very nice man. I mean, he seems like a very nice man."

Madeline made a disparaging gesture. "I daresay that he is. I find him a good deal too much like a sheep. He only blushes and stammers and makes foolish compliments." She noticed Isabella's frown. "Now, Bella, I know that you cannot bear for a bad word to be said about anyone. I am sorry. I only mean that we could not suit, and I wish he did not admire me quite so much. Now you must forgive me; I have many more pressing things than Sir George to attend to."

"Lambrook has not proposed—"

"No, and I am glad he did not. I would have had to plant him a facer." Madeline viciously pummeled a cushion again for illustration.

"You do not love him?" Isabella was obviously disappointed that this drama straight from the covers of a Minerva Press novel was lacking in several key romantic elements.

"Of course not, you goose! I had only just met him!"

"Then why did you do it?"

"I don't know," Madeline said thoughtfully, tucking her feet up under her. "That is the worst of it. I only did it to find out what it was like to flaunt the rules and to be kissed and things like that. But the entire situation has gotten entirely out of control. I think it could have been a thousand times worse. You would think I murdered the man, the way everyone is carrying on. It was just a kiss. And I did not even enjoy it," she added softly.

"Would you have married him if he had asked?"

Madeline felt her face warm slightly at the memory of the morning's disastrous interview with Lambrook. She decided it would only shock Isabella into fits to hear of it. "I suppose I would have. I would hardly have had any choice. At first I thought I wanted to. I thought it might be nice to be a married lady and not have all the silly rules that we have to attend to. But, in retrospect, I have decided I am glad he did not propose as I am certain we would not suit."

"Well," Isabella said doubtfully, "I do not think it was all *that* scandalous. It is only said that you waltzed with him, and that it was indiscreet of you. No one knows about that . . . that other part." She blushed again. "Perhaps you are not so very ruined after all. Perhaps this will be forgotten, and no lasting damage will have been done."

"That is not what Papa thinks." Madeline gave the pillow another thump. "He acts as though I was caught *in delicto* with the man."

"Madeline!" Isabella went pale.

Her friend rolled her eyes comically. "Well, it hardly matters now. I am off to the country to spend time with my beastly cousin Frederick."

"How dreadful!"

"Yes, I will languish away while everyone here is having a good time. It is quite a Gothic banishment. Perhaps I shall go into a decline." She laughed at herself and pretended that she was not heartbroken.

"Mis-ter Fooooooooorrrrrth!" Devin heard Frederick's wail and characteristic thumping up the stairs long before he actually saw him.

"What is wrong?" Devin asked as the boy flew into the room and grabbed him by the cuff.

"Hide me!" Frederick released him and dove into a cupboard.

Devin stood for a moment, listening to the lad bumping around in the dark of his hiding place. "Freddie," he said calmly, "who are you hiding from?"

"Monster girl! Mad Maddie!" came the muffled reply, followed by a marked increase in noise.

"Who is Mad Maddie?"

"Cousin Maddie." Frederick's head appeared from the cupboard. "She is coming here because the season made her sick. At least that is what Mama said. I think it was because no one wanted to marry her. Nanny said she was coming out here to rust because of some scandal. Do you think she is really going to rust?" This prospect appeared to please Frederick immensely.

"I doubt it." Devin suppressed a smile. "Furthermore, I think you can rest assured that she will not hound you." He guessed correctly that Frederick rather enjoyed the attention he received from his cousin, even if it did involve being subjected to her pranks.

The boy did not have any friends of his own age and spent most of his time with his old nursery maid or with Devin himself. He was pleased that this young relation was coming to provide more amusement for Frederick than he ever could. However, she was several years older than Freddie, and these were years in which a girl changes into a young woman with definite ideas about fraternizing with ten-year-old cousins.

"Young misses in their first season are very unlikely to want to have anything to do with their cousins who are still in the schoolroom," he commented wryly to Frederick, pretending to pacify him, but intending to warn him that Cousin Maddie might not be the same as he remembered. The boy made an exaggerated sigh of relief and climbed out of his hiding place. "And to make sure that *you* are not tempted to hound *her*, I will see that you are very busy with a long Latin assignment."

The boy wrinkled his nose in response. "Do you think she is really sick?" he asked at last.

"I suppose we will have to wait and see." Devin found that he was indeed anxious to meet this hellion cousin who held such fascination for his young charge.

"Madeline darling, we are so delighted that you are here at last. Your father wrote to tell us of your coming. Poor dear, I had no idea the rigors of the season would wreck such a healthy constitution as yours." Lady Hesstrow made hen noises and fluttered about her niece.

"I assure you, Aunt Enid, I am feeling much better already." Madeline smiled, kissing her aunt on the cheek.

"Oh, dear"—that lady pressed her hand to the cheek her niece had kissed— "you are certain that it is nothing contagious? You know how susceptible I am . . ." Lady Hesstrow was a confirmed hypochondriac.

"No, no. It is only fatigue," Madeline reassured her. "You remember my companion, Mrs. Benjamin?"

"Of course, of course. You are very welcome here, Mrs. Benjamin." Lady Hesstrow and Mrs. Benjamin treated each other to sugared smiles. Their mutual hatred had begun three years ago over a heated discussion regarding whose family headache poultice was the most effective.

Madeline heard a pounding noise on the stairs and turned to see her cousin making a dramatic descent. He stopped at the bottom of the flight and stared rudely at her.

"Now, here is Frederick," his mother announced. "Frederick, say hello to your cousin Madeline."

" 'Lo," the boy replied, looking her over with interest. "I see why no one wanted to marry you. Your dresses are far too fluffy."

"Frederick! Mind your manners!" Lady Hesstrow snapped. Madeline ignored him with what she hoped was an air of cool sophistication.

"Mother, Mr. Forth says I am finished with lessons. May I please go out on my pony?"

"Frederick, no. We will be having luncheon now, and you will be served in the schoolroom with Mr. Forth. After that, perhaps you may ride." Frederick's mouth turned down in a pout.

"Why does Madeline get to eat with everyone and I don't?" he demanded.

"Because I am not a little cretin," Madeline retorted before she could stop herself.

Lady Hesstrow's brows rose in surprise, but Frederick responded by sticking out his tongue and pulling his nose into a pig snout. Madeline barely refrained from responding in kind and managed to sigh in derision. Frederick pounded up the stairs with as much venom as he could muster. He found his tutor laughing at the top of the flight. "Do you see what I mean?" Frederick asked, with a comic expression of utter disgust.

"I certainly do." Devin smiled ruefully.

Three

"Of course you will think that Elmhurst is quite flat after all the excitement of London," Lady Hesstrow said petulantly as she picked at the food on her plate. "Do take some of the turtle soup. Our cook is considered excellent, you know. He is French, of course. Though I must have a word with him; I did not think the jugged hares were quite as nice yesterday as they have been on previous occasions." She allowed the footman to refill her glass of wine. "Do you like the wine?"

"Indeed, it is excellent," Madeline replied.

Lady Hesstrow scrutinized her glass. "It is passable. You know, of course, that we are considered quite the social leaders in our community. Lord Hesstrow is a dear friend of Lord Taunton himself, aren't you Edmund?"

"Went to Eton together," her uncle replied.

"Indeed, and the Stantons visit us nearly every year when they are on their way from Town to their country home. Indeed I would almost say that we are fashionable. Would you not agree, Edmund?"

"Indeed," he said mildly, pressing green peas into the scalloped potatoes piled on the back of his fork. "How is Albert?" he asked Madeline gruffly.

"Very well, thank you. He sends all of you his fondest regards."

"We have not seen Albert in such a long time. Of course, he is always inviting us up to London, but my health . . . Lady Hesstrow pressed a hand to her ample bosom. "I declare, I should not like to live in London. Too noisy by far. If I had a daughter I would of course be obliged to bring her out in some style, but otherwise, we are quite well set up here."

"Hate London," her uncle announced.

"Indeed, Edmund positively detests London. Yes, I don't believe anything could entice us to go there. Of course, I do have my modistes come from there. Do you know Madame Henri? She is outrageously expensive because the creature insists on coming post when I daresay the mail would be quite good enough for her. But then, I suppose she is quite knowledgeable as to French fashions, and she really is worth every shilling. Who is your modiste, my dear?"

"Mrs. Harper."

"Not a Frenchwoman; really, my dear!" Lady Hesstrow shook her head and scowled at Mrs. Benjamin. "Indeed, at times like these you must really feel the loss of your poor dear mother. I am sure she would have wanted you to have a French modiste."

Madeline refrained from telling her aunt that Madame Henri was no more French than Mrs. Harper. "I think, Aunt, that I will go up to my room and lie down. I have a bit of a headache after the journey."

"Do you, my dear?"

Madeline saw the martial light in her aunt's eye and instantly regretted feigning that particular malady.

"Well, run upstairs and I will send up some of my tisane. I know how much it soothed you when you were here last."

Madeline fled the room as Mrs. Benjamin visibly bristled.

She was relieved to be alone after the tedium of the trip and her aunt's interminable need to prove how very fashionable they were despite the fact that they lived in the country. The solitude of her room quickly lost its charm too, so she decided she would be more amused by exploring the rambling old home where her mother had grown up and the Hesstrow family had lived for generations. It was a very old house that had been added to in times of prosperity and now boasted an entirely refurbished ballroom and very modern kitchen. Other rooms, however, were rarely used anymore, and several wings of the upper floors were shut off entirely, as her uncle's household was very small.

Madeline roamed along a gallery hung with portraits of her ancestors. She stopped in front of each one and scrutinized the subject's clothing and expression. Occasionally she touched her own face, as if to try to feel if there was any resemblance between these people and herself. She had heard that she resembled her mother, yet indeed, all of the portraits appeared to have her own oval face and wide-set eyes. Most had fair hair and blue eyes, but they ranged from a pale watery blue to the deep blue of her own.

"You must have been the most terrible rake," she announced to a man in an enormous neck ruff, with scowling brows over very un-Hesstrowlike black eyes. I am surprised you ever married. Perhaps you didn't. Perhaps you are only a younger brother who was killed in a duel."

This scenario pleased her, and she moved on to the next picture. It featured a woman gazing fondly at her two plump children. The children appeared to be very serious and didn't look as though they could be nearly as loud as Frederick. She wondered what they had grown up to be like and if they had ever done anything horrible enough to be banished from London to this forsaken place. These children appeared so insipid, they probably were not capable of anything more than picking the flowers they held so daintily between their fat little fingers.

She came at last to a portrait of her mother and studied it intently. She looked like a kind-enough woman, but as Madeline had no memory of her, she was not particularly moved by the artist's rather indifferent rendition of her parent. Wandering on, she found a salon with its furniture swathed in Holland covers. The room was crowded with pieces of a different era, and a pianoforte stood along one wall. It was sadly out of tune, but she played a few songs on it anyway, morosely enjoying the bizarre discordance.

"You play terribly," a voice announced. She jumped at the sound and whirled around. A tall man stood in the doorway, smiling.

"It's you!"

"It's you," Devin echoed in shock. Abruptly, his mouth quirked wryly to the left side.

"What are you doing here?" she demanded. Shame made her heart pound as though she had been running. She slammed the pianoforte cover over the keys with more force than she had intended, and the strings protested with a jarring twang.

"I . . . live here." He had been relaxed when she first saw him, but now he drew himself up into that disapproving stance she remembered so well from the day he had walked her home from Watier's.

"You live with the Hesstrows?" she repeated in confusion.

"I am Frederick's tutor." He crossed his arms across his chest and looked defiant.

"Oh." Madeline could not think of a suitable reply. How provoking that he should be here. She should have guessed he was a tutor, but he was even more prudish and dull than most. "I am Frederick's cousin. My name is Madeline Delaney, in case you do not recall." She raised a brow at him and dared him to comment. He merely regarded her with some interest. At last she sighed resolutely and continued. "As you doubtless have guessed, I am here to learn the error of my reckless ways, so you needn't launch into another of your lectures on propriety."

"Please forgive my insufferability on that occasion." He smiled, and she noticed that his eyes crinkled in a nice way. "I was not in the best of tempers for unrelated reasons that day." He seemed to be regarding her with a speculation that contained a teasing mockery. "I am Devin Forth, in case *you* do not recall. I am charmed to make your acquaintance." He shook her hand solemnly, but his graygreen eyes had a suspicious gleam. Madeline thought she had heard him murmur, "Mad Maddie under his breath, but that was impossible.

"What did you say?"

"I apologize madam, I was simply expressing my gratitude that you have come to make things a little more exciting around here . . . for Frederick."

She was still piqued that his presence at Elmhurst would be a constant reminder of one of her more humiliating adventures. Surely his discretion could be relied upon . . . "Well, I am hardly here for Frederick's amusement," she retorted with asperity. "I'm ill." She knew, however, with the flush of color that accompanied her anger, she hardly looked the part.

"No more climbing out of windows, then," he retorted cheerfully.

"I never! Well, I certainly wouldn't now. I'm out now." She resisted the urge to stamp her foot.

"My apologies," he returned contritely. "I misunderstood." He looked directly at her in a way that made her long to say something cutting, but as she could think of nothing witty enough, she contented herself with sweeping past him with a sniff of derision.

"I will thank you not to be so familiar with me in the future. I am sure my aunt would not like me to associate with her servants." She regretted the words as soon as she had spoken them. Nothing she could have said would have been more hurtful. After all, he was obviously a gentleman, and tutors were not servants. She looked at him, stricken.

Forth drew himself up stiffly as though she had slapped him. He suddenly seemed very tall, and the angular planes of his face took on a very threatening appearance. Madeline drew back.

"Of course, madam," he said with mocking obsequiousness. He gave a half-bow.

"I didn't mean that," she pleaded. She had been on the point of passing him at the doorway when she had insulted him, but now she retired nearly to the middle of the room.

He did not reply.

"I only meant that I hope you do not mention the circumstances under which we met before." She was annoyed to hear that her voice had gotten very high and small. Devin now approached her. It took all of her courage to stand her ground and not dart in cowardice behind a piece of furniture. He stopped only when he was directly in front of her. Although he did not touch her, she felt transfixed as though he had pinioned her by the arms.

"But you know how indiscreet servants can be," he said quietly, his eyes unblinking.

"It is only that everyone would be quite upset if they knew how disastrous that little adventure was."

"Quite upset."

"You are not attempting to blackmail me, are you, Mr. Forth?" She found that she could not look into his face, but focused only on his cravat.

"I could." He stepped even closer. Madeline noticed in a disoriented manner that he smelled rather nice. "But only a widgeon like you would think of something so Gothic. I will settle for an agreement that we avoid each other as much as possible. I have enough on my hands, what with keeping your cousin Frederick out of trouble. I do not need to play nursery maid to you. I would rather not have to come to rescue you from the consequences of your addlepated notions." His scowl deepened. "That ridiculous hat!"

"It was all I had!" she protested, suppressing an urge to laugh as the farcical side of the situation struck her, "I didn't want to be recognized!"

"You would have been less conspicuous if you had walked naked down the street."

She blushed and dropped her eyes again to his cravat. She wondered what he would have thought of her if she had. It couldn't have been worse than his opinion now.

"How surprising, a maidenly blush," he said with sarcasm. Madeline stepped away from him, hurt by this jab, and her movement seemed to remind him of propriety. "You will stay away from me," he commanded.

"Gladly." Madeline escaped the room at a pace that was almost a run. Rage and shame swept over her, but she forced herself to keep walking. Once she was back in her room, it was a long time before she finished stalking about and muttering unladylike curses under her breath. This was beyond anything. How was it that this man seemed to catch her at her worst moments? She threw herself into a chair to catch her breath.

She knew she should never have even spoken to him. She should have stared down his incivilities with a cold eye. But something about the way he spoke to her made her forget her dignity. It was infuriating. She caught a glimpse of herself in the dressing table mirror. Parts of her hair had fallen down, and her dress was covered in a fine powdering of dust. She looked like a child—a dirty ragamuffin child at that.

She wondered what her London beaux would say if they saw her now. If they knew she had climbed out of a window on bedsheets three years ago. . . . If they knew she had hunted down a gentleman, wearing a black cape and that silly yellow hat two weeks ago. . . . If they knew she was ruined. But, doubtless, they did know that.

Her thoughts drifted again to Mr. Forth. It was too bad that beastly little Frederick had told him about the window incident. Forth seemed to only know about her more humiliating escapades. It was unfortunate that she had lost her temper and said what she did, but the man really was insufferably bold. He was a good deal too young to be a tutor anyway. Were they not supposed to be hawk-nosed and bent with age?

She knew tutors and governesses held a strange place in the hierarchy of the household. In some homes, they were treated like family members or guests and took dinner with the family and were included in social events. In others, they were merely servants who were treated as though they had neither senses nor feelings.

Mrs. Benjamin, her nanny and later her governess, was more a mother to her than anything. Benny was never ever treated as a servant and was allowed every liberty. Somehow that man was different. Such an arrogant and pompous incivility! Really, her aunt should never have let such a man in the house. He was a good deal too upsetting, and probably put the chambermaids into fits. What a way to begin her wretched exile.

It was several days later that her aunt Enid remembered Madeline's presence and called her into her rooms where she was reclining on a settee, a box of expensive comfits, nearby. "Madeline. I hope you are doing well?" she asked.

"I do hope the potion I sent up the other afternoon cured you of the headache. It is an old family recipe, you know. Absolutely unrivaled in its ability to cure headaches. I never get them myself, and you know how delicate I am."

Madeline nodded, declining to explain that she had a genuine headache from spending most of the last two days hidden in her room and reading illicit romance novels.

Enid went on. "As you know, we are fortunate here at Elmhurst to be considered one of the first families in the neighborhood. We are often in the habit of entertaining hunting parties made up of very tonnish families from Town."

She obviously wanted to impress upon her niece that residing in the country did not make them rustics. She lovingly smoothed the skirts of her fashionable gown. Madeline privately thought Madame Henri's creation a good deal too fine for day wear in the country, but she only nodded and smiled.

Lady Hesstrow wanted little encouragement to continue. "I know that you have recently arrived here to recover from the extravagance and excesses of the season, but I cannot allow you to forgo your social duty. You must learn to be strong and to keep up social obligations." Here, she scowled at Madeline, who had some small idea of where this lecture was leading. "We feel, that is, Lord Hesstrow and I feel, it is *our* social obligation as hosts to entertain you and to continue to uphold our responsibility to our neighbors by sponsoring social events." She smiled resolutely, as though this were a burdensome duty indeed.

"I understand, Lady Hesstrow," Madeline replied.

"I intend to have a small party, with dancing, in a week. Your health will bear it." She said this as more of a command than a question.

"Yes, ma'am." Madeline managed to keep a straight face.

"I shall engage Madame Henri to come down from London to make my gown. Do you have one that will do, or will you need another? You do look very young." Enid peered at her critically. "Well, there is no helping that. Perhaps we can get Madame Henri to create something for you that will help you look older . . . and taller."

Madeline longed to snap back that she had never had any criticism of her looks or her height in London. However, there was no arguing with the woman.

"Perhaps you play the pianoforte?" Lady Hesstrow continued.

"Not well, Aunt," she admitted with a blush, recalling the laughing remark of Frederick's tutor. She had not seen him again.

"Well, I suppose we shall have to ask Cornelia Wylie's daughter, as she plays very well. Thank heavens, she is plain," Enid mused. "You dance, I suppose."

"I had a dancing instructor at my finishing school."

"Well, I shall ask Frederick's tutor to act as your dancing master."

"No!" The word was out of her mouth at a shockingly loud volume before she had time to think.

"Whyever not?"

"I met him . . . I didn't like him. He was . . . impertinent," she explained incoherently, angrily aware that her cheeks were becoming flushed. She suddenly realized it was possible the tutor would be dismissed on account of her complaint. She immediately tried to explain. "It is only . . . I mean he . . . Well I think I am proficient enough in dancing, and I do not need a dancing master."

"Nonsense. You will begin after luncheon." Enid waved a languid hand to dismiss her protests. "Now, dear, why don't you read to me while I rest my poor eyes? They are piteously strained." She instantly assumed an invalid's position on the lounge and dramatically pressed a hand to her eyes.

Madeline sighed at an almost audible volume, then picked up a book of Hannah More's sermons. It didn't really matter what she read, since Lady Hesstrow was always asleep in two minutes. She had always wanted to read one of her more thrilling gothic romances aloud, just to see if the woman noticed. As predicted, her aunt's "eye resting" quickly turned to gentle snores, and Madeline put down the book and crept from the room.

"Bother," she muttered with a scowl. "If I am going to have to deal with that man, I may as well go tell him that it was not my idea. Doubtless he will think it was some conniving on my part to torture him."

She mounted the stairs to the schoolroom. At the second floor she stopped and looked into the glass to make sure she did not resemble the dirty, scraggly child she had seemed on their last meeting. Her Pomona green dress was fashionably cut and not so frilly as some of her other gowns. It deepened her blue eyes to indigo. She drew herself up to her full height and assumed an expression of what she hoped was well-bred maturity.

Her heart pounded as she neared the schoolroom door, but she dismissed it as due to the exertion of stair-climbing and the lack of exercise over the last few days. She found Frederick sitting at his desk and tracing trade routes onto a map while his tutor looked over the boy's shoulder. They both looked up and saw her.

"Cousin Madeline!" Frederick exclaimed with a great deal more enthusiasm than he had shown at their first meeting. "My cousin has come to see me, Mr. Forth. May we stop lessons?"

"Oh, no. I didn't mean to interrupt. I shall come back later," Madeline protested. She suddenly decided it was a silly idea to apologize, only likely to make that bear of a man more cross.

"But it would be so rude to keep going." Frederick was suspiciously insistent on stopping the lesson. He shot an assessing look at Mr. Forth.

"Well, Frederick, perhaps we can incorporate Miss Delaney's arrival into our lesson." His sardonic smile and the quirk of one dark brow let her know that she had not been forgiven. "Miss Delaney can give us a lesson in social history. Certainly she can tell us the cost of each of her dresses, divided by the inheritance of each man who has admired them. Perhaps she will regale us with the family history and approximate monetary expectations of every peer of marriageable age in London. It is required knowledge for young ladies in their first season." His gray eyes flashed menacingly.

Madeline bridled and almost turned around and left the room. Then she changed her mind and gave him a dazzling smile as she walked to the front of it. "Well, I know everything about everyone who is anyone," she replied pertly. "I shall start at the top." She folded her hands and stared into the middle distance as she recited in a high and lisping voice: "Lord Edgewood is eligible, but slightly old at forty-two. He is exceedingly wealthy, with expectations of approximately eighty thousand a year, but shows no interest in women at all. Lord Mealington-Smythe is young and wealthy, with an income of approximately sixty-four thousand per annum, but insanity and impotency run in his family.

"Lord Farnsworth is poor and ugly, but very well connected. He just might wrangle a land gift from Prinny himself as they are quite bosom bows these days. However Farnsworth, is expected to announce his engagement to Miss Elizabeth Hound-sheath at any moment. Lord Lambrook is heavily financially encumbered through gaming and is received in only a handful of houses as he is a rake and would ruin a girl without proposing." She felt a pang as she said this and could not look at Forth, but continued on rapidly.

"Viscount Hodskins is moderately rich, with an income of four thousand a year, moderately old at thirty-seven, terribly ugly and drinks to excess. I believe he is considered a four-bottle man. Viscount Weatherby is so poor that he is ineligible. Sir Billings is fat and has gout, but is very kindly and excessively wealthy. I have heard seventy thousand, but I am not certain. Sir Robert Tattford is moderately well off, but his father is a spendthrift and may go through it all before young Tattford inherits. Lord Brandon, Lord Willis, and Sir Bedford-Penny are all engaged, and Mr. Geoffry Allen is perhaps the wealthiest of all, but his ancestors were in trade and he is a mere mister." She finished this breakneck-speed recitation and looked with insouciance at Mr. Forth. "Shall I go on?"

"Very impressive, Miss Delaney," he acquiesced with a laugh.

"You went too fast," Frederick objected.

"Thank you." She laughed at herself. "I actually came up here to speak about my dancing lessons, but perhaps I should wait until after you have finished this lesson."

"Dancing lessons?"

"You see, my aunt feels I should have dancing lessons and that you should teach them."

Forth looked unpleasantly surprised.

"It was not *my* idea," she added quickly. Involuntarily, she entertained the thought of this handsome man partnering her as they floated across the dance floor, while he murmured the sequence of the steps for her ears alone.

"No, I am certain it was not." The tutor arched a brow. "You would have insisted on importing a dancing master from Italy. Lady Hesstrow seems to think I am a servant of all trades." His eyes glittered dangerously.

Madeline flinched as he emphasized the word "servant" for her benefit.

"Frederick," Mr. Forth continued with deceptive calmness. "You may put away your maps, and we shall talk a moment about the dancing lessons. You are young yet, but your mother feels it is not too soon for you to begin some formal lessons in dancing, especially since your cousin is here to partner you."

"What?" Frederick and Madeline chorused in horror.

"Aunt Enid did not mention Frederick!"

"I don't want to learn to dance!" Frederick shouted above her protests. "I want to learn to hunt! What is the point of learning to dance? I never want to go to any stupid balls anyway." Frederick began to look murderously sulky.

"Nonsense," replied Mr. Forth firmly. "I am certain Lady Hesstrow would not want her own son to be left out of the dancing lessons. Doubtless, she intended from the start that you should both learn. As for you, Frederick, your father has promised to take you out hunting this fall, and you shall have many opportunities to learn the more manly skills. However, dancing is a skill you will also learn, like it or not; and it is better to learn now rather than later when you are more easily made a fool of. Besides"—here he darted a triumphant look at Madeline—"your cousin is only slightly taller than you and is certain to be a fairly accomplished dancer already."

Madeline wanted to howl that this was not fair. Mr. Forth was undoubtably right. Her aunt planned to force her to spend her time playing partner to some clumsy boy who would doubtless take forever to learn anything, while she herself would learn nothing new. She held her tongue, however, when she saw that Mr. Forth was watching her closely, daring her to make another unladylike scene. She smiled and nodded graciously. "I am certain it will be a pleasure," she managed to choke out at last and then got up to lead the way to luncheon.

Four

Mrs. Benjamin had been recruited to play the piano and to act as chaperone for the lessons. They began somewhat later after luncheon than had been anticipated, as Frederick had to be found and dragged bodily back into the house from his hiding place in the stables. The peculiar quartet stood at last in the second-best drawing room with the late afternoon sun streaming in the windows.

After first explaining the basic steps to a simple reel, Mr. Forth took Madeline by the hand and carefully demonstrated how a man should partner a woman through the sequence. Madeline was surprised by the warmth of his hand and the ease with which he guided her through the figure. How nice it would be to be naturally graceful.

"Very nice," he commented at last when they were done.

Frederick sighed audibly and rolled his eyes. "Do we have to do this?"

"Yes. No matter how unpleasant."

Madeline could not tell if Mr. Forth was referring to her or not. She reminded herself that she was not going to make a scene and schooled her features into pleasant lines. Frederick reluctantly came forward and took Madeline's hand as Devin had done. As the tutor clapped and counted, and Mrs. Benjamin played the reel at a dirgelike speed, she and her cousin moved laboriously through the figures.

Frederick squeezed her hand tightly so that her rings pressed painfully into her fingers. She smiled placidly and planted her foot squarely on top of his. Frederick howled and was preparing to respond in kind when Mr. Forth stepped in.

"Enough, children," he said sarcastically. "Miss Delaney, I expect you to act with a little more restraint and not stoop to this child's play."

Madeline wanted to protest, but regarded him with composure instead. It was obvious he was attempting to humiliate her. Without complaint, she dutifully partnered Frederick for the remainder of the lesson, patiently enduring his heavy footfalls, damp palms, and inability to tell his right from his left.

At last they adjourned. Frederick, who had been so lackluster, was now full of energy. "Can I go outside, Mr. Forth?" Devin nodded, and the lad nearly ran to the door. "Come on, Maddie!" He shouted, "We are free! Come see my fort in the woods. It is two stories tall, and it has a rope to swing from!" He had instantly forgotten their quarrel, apparently regarding it as not only expected but necessary.

Madeline hesitated. She had given up such childish pastimes long ago, and was much too old to go romping in the woods with her cousin. It was strangely tempting, though. She realized how long it had been since she had done something that did not involve following a strict code of rules. Well, that was not strictly true. She had flaunted the rules quite a bit of late.

"No, thank you, Frederick," she replied, "but thank you for asking."

"But you must! Don't be boring like everyone else." He made a gesture to include Mrs. Benjamin and his tutor.

"I will, but not right now. I am wearing all the wrong clothes for it." She smiled cajolingly.

"You think you are such a grown-up, Maddie, but you aren't. You are just dull!" Frederick was obviously cross with her defection.

"I am sorry, but I would rather see it another time." She was very aware that Mr. Forth's eyes were upon her, judging her reaction.

"Oh, I have to go and play with my pretty clothes!" Her cousin imitated her in a high, squeaky voice. "I have to practice being fast." He fluttered his eyelashes furiously. "I have to get someone to marry me!" His voice returned to normal. "No one will ever want to marry you, Maddie! You are not fast enough!"

Madeline let out a whoop of shocked laughter, but Forth scowled.

"Frederick!" He clapped a hand on the boy's shoulder. "You will not speak to your cousin like that. I know you are excited that she is here, but you must realize she is a young lady now and may not share all of your interests as she once did. She has been very patient in dancing with you, especially when she is quite an accomplished dancer and does not really need lessons." Mr. Forth turned Frederick to face Madeline and regarded her solemnly himself. "Tell her that you are sorry you have been so rude," he said quietly.

Frederick may have mumbled the words, but Madeline did not notice. She was looking at his tutor and struggling to control a sudden shortness of breath that seemed to be a belated aftereffect of dancing.

Although it would have been considered terribly unfashionable in London, Madeline arose before anyone else. She felt restless, and after pacing her room for a while and starting several letters to Isabella, she decided to go for a ride on the mare Lord Hesstrow had recently procured for her.

"Shall I saddle up Daisy for you, miss?" the groom asked cheerfully when he saw her.

"Yes, please. Which one is Daisy?"

"This sprightly young thing right here." He patted the nose of a mare who pranced about in a delighted response. "Lord Hesstrow said you liked a horse with a bit of spirit."

Madeline eyed her with some misgivings. "Oh, well, I suppose I did say something like that." She thought of the swaybacked old pony her father kept at his country estate.

"Well, Daisy here's a sweet goer. What sort of mount did you keep up in Town?"

"Um . . . brown?" she hazarded.

The groom looked at her for a moment before bursting into uproarious laughter. "Good one, miss. Very good one. Well, your uncle's a devout hunter and you can trust him to be a good judge of horseflesh. This mare is a clever one. She knows all the tricks."

That was just what Madeline was afraid of. She resolutely mounted, however, and set off, a groom following unobtrusively behind. They were still within sight of the stable when her arms began to ache with the strain of holding Daisy back to a walk. She was just beginning to doubt the wisdom of this venture and to consider turning home again, when she heard her name called and saw Mr. Forth appear on horseback over the crest of a hill.

Reining Daisy in with an effort, she watched as Mr. Forth approached. He looked upsettingly dashing in a deep gray riding jacket. She had determined at last, late the night before, that she would be kind to him, but would keep her distance and remind him of his station if an uncomfortable moment arose. Mr. Forth looked calm and rode with the ease of great experience.

"Miss Delaney, I did not know you rode," he began.

Unwilling to admit that her prowess in this

arena was less than she herself had previously hoped, she smiled and replied with something noncommittal. "But I see that you do," she continued brightly, surprised that her aunt and uncle were so generous as to provide a mount for their son's tutor.

"Indeed. The Hesstrows are kind enough to let me keep my horse at their stables," he replied just as though she had asked. "I often ride out in the mornings before lessons with Frederick. I am surprised that you are out so early."

"I could not sleep in." Madeline could not help smiling warmly. The day was so fine, and Mr. Forth seemed to be in such a good humor. The distant sound of a shot made Daisy jump.

"Do be careful. It is only a poacher or some such thing, you know. Your uncle allows the tenants to do some hunting on the sly as long as they don't take the young animals. They are quite far away, so there is no need to be anxious. I do hope your horse is not prone to startle."

"I have her well in hand." Madeline smiled, hoping the strain did not show on her face. "You ride very well," she commented enviously.

"Thank you. My family used to have many superior horses," he replied. "My sisters, however, are terrible horsewomen. They seem to think that riding is only a chance to show off how well they look in a riding habit."

She laughed a little too loudly, glancing down at her own indigo wool habit. She was proud of it, feeling that it complemented her eyes and brightened the gold in her hair, but she would rather die than admit that now.

"That is a fine hat," Forth remarked wickedly, indicating the feathered creation she wore rakishly tilted over one brow. "Much more becoming than the yellow one."

"It is positively evil of you to comment on that incident," Madeline replied, repressing a laugh. "I refuse to speak of it. You must tell me instead of how you came to Elmhurst from London. You are from there, I suppose?"

"No, I was only there for about a week to see Mr. Wren, my solicitor. My father died almost a year ago, and I was belatedly seeing to his affairs. I am from Somerton, not a half-day's ride from here."

"I noticed that you were in mourning the day I met you. I am sorry for your loss."

He acknowledged her comment with a nod. "My father's brother married Lady Hesstrow's sister," he continued, "but I do not like to trespass upon the Hesstrows' generosity so much that I should step out of my chosen station here at Elmhurst. My father was a younger son who made a very good match in love, though very poor in dowry. His father, the Earl of Somerton, disowned him entirely."

"The Earl of Somerton?" she repeated in surprise.

"Indeed," he said coolly. "Does that impress you?"

"Don't get cross with me, Mr. Forth," she said

cajolingly. "You know very well it does not impress me. Please do tell me how you came to be here at Elmhurst."

"I have taken the post as tutor here because Lord Hesstrow offered it to me, along with a rather outrageously generous salary, so that I may have my independence."

"I had wondered why you were treated so differently than the rest of the . . . household." Madeline blushed furiously. She would not dare use the word servant, but he was not a guest either.

She did not have time to assess Mr. Forth's reaction to her imprudent comment. A second shot rang out over the next dale. It was far off, but Daisy started violently and pulled the reins out of her tired hands. The horse sprang into a gallop, with a leap that nearly dislodged her from the saddle, and began to bolt down the hill they had ascended. It happened so quickly, she did not have time to do anything but cry out in surprise and wildly clutch the mare's mane to keep her seat. She was vaguely aware of hoofbeats behind her and of the shouts of Mr. Forth and the groom.

"Miss Delaney! Hold on! I'll stop her!" She could hear Forth's voice close behind her. Just as he drew abreast of her and was attempting to catch the bridle of the terrified horse, Daisy stumbled, and Madeline went flying into the heather.

She landed on her back with such force the breath was knocked out of her, and she could only lie there, stunned, for a moment. Forth yelped a curse and flung himself from the saddle.

"Oh, my God, Madeline!" He dropped to his knees beside her and looked desperately into her face.

"I am all right," she managed to gasp, hoping it was true. It crossed her mind vaguely that he had called her by her first name.

"Can you move? Where does it hurt?"

"Really, I am fine. I just—oof—I just want to lie here a moment." He obligingly let her lie with her eyes closed until Daisy plodded over, panting, to see how her mistress fared. The horse breathed heavily into her face. "Oh, Daisy, you monstrous beast, how could you do that to me?" she chided, heaving herself into a sitting position. The groom had now arrived and helped Mr. Forth assist her to her feet. Overall, she was unhurt, only bruised and winded from the fall.

"Would you like to mount again, or shall we walk home?" he inquired solicitously, his formal demeanor regained.

"I . . . I think I would rather walk." She paused. "I am so embarrassed at the spectacle I have just made. You must think me a featherwit, Mr. Forth. I must thank you for your heroic rescue."

"It is not often that I have a chance to do something so dashing," he admitted with a warm laugh. "Come, take my arm. It is a long way back, and I am afraid you must be tired."

They walked on for a while, leading their mounts while the groom followed. Forth's arm was strong, and Madeline enjoyed leaning close against him. Occasionally she allowed her cheek to brush against the fabric of his coat sleeve. She recalled with pleasure the concern in his voice and the way he had looked at her. She must have appeared the veriest fool after the fall, but he was most kind about it. "Were you worried?" she asked without preamble.

"Very! I will never forgive myself for not paying better attention."

"You called me Madeline," she ventured, looking at him shyly from underneath her lashes.

Devin stiffened slightly. His warmth and friendliness seemed to evaporate in an instant. "Forgive me, Miss Delaney."

"I do not mind." She smiled encouragingly.

"I beg your pardon, but I do not think that would be proper." He was instantly the pompous man she remembered from that rainy day in London. They walked for some way in silence. "You should have told your uncle to give you a mount suitable for a beginner," he said gruffly. She did not reply. "You should never have been mounted on a horse you could not handle. If you had fallen and killed yourself, I would have been to blame."

"Is that all you care about?" she demanded peevishly. Her bones were beginning to ache, and this dreadful man was certainly not being properly attentive. At least he could be a little more sympathetic instead of prosing on about propriety as he always seemed to do.

"You should learn to be more responsible. Racing off in such a madcap way was simply inexcusable. I am sure you never gave thought to the grief you would have caused your aunt and uncle by having an accident. It was simply thoughtless and reckless of you to put yourself at such risk."

"I will thank you, Mr. Forth, not to lecture me as though I were Frederick. You know very well it was not my fault the horse bolted," she snapped.

"You are more trouble than Frederick," he returned nastily.

"I am not your responsibility."

"I pity the man whose responsibility you are." Forth scowled at her, but seeing that she winced with every step, he sighed and swept her into his arms.

"Stop it! How dare you! I can walk on my own!" Madeline twisted about in protest, but found the movement too painful. Forth looked stonily ahead and ignored her rants. There was nothing to do but suffer the ignominy of being carried to the house like a rag doll.

For the rest of the week, Madeline nursed her aches and bruises and a curious heaviness in her chest. As she could not attend dancing lessons, she had not seen Mr. Forth, and he had not come to visit her. She alternately felt embarrassed at the entire humiliating incident and annoyed that he had taken her to task for it when it was not her fault.

"How are you feeling my dear?" Lady Hesstrow

bustled into the room carrying salve, while Mrs. Benjamin followed with a meal on a tray. Her aunt had instantly cast herself into the role of chief nurse, to Mrs. Benjamin's annoyance.

"Better, I suppose."

"Oh, what a horrible thing to have happened! I could kill Edmund for giving you such a wild horse! Oh! I never ride myself. Never at all."

Madeline closed her eyes. Lady Hesstrow had had this conversation with herself at least three or four times a day since the accident.

"I have brought you your salve. I know how it eases your pain. I think it should be the *only* salve you should use from now on." She shot a dagger look at Mrs. Benjamin.

"You are very kind, Aunt. I wish that you would not put yourself out taking care of me. I know you are busy with preparations for the party."

"You will be well enough to attend?" Lady Hesstrow's brow furrowed.

"Yes, I believe so."

"Good heavens, I nearly thought everything was ruined. Thank the Lord, Mr. Forth was there!" Enid said, tut-tutting and shaking her head as she vigorously plumped the pillows.

"He saved your life, you know," she announced dramatically. "Oh, thank heaven's he was there. I don't know what we would have told your father if you had been killed." With this dramatic pronouncement, she swept out of the room, leaving Mrs. Benjamin to scowl after her.

"How are you, pet?" she asked, insinuating that

Madeline could tell the truth now that Lady Hesstrow was gone.

"Really, I am better." Madeline forced herself to smile. Of course, Mr. Forth had not saved her life, but he had tried to help her. Devin. That was a nice name. Devin. It was a pity the man was so moody, she reminded herself.

"I hope you will be well enough for the party," Mrs. Benjamin said.

"Of course I will." Madeline got up and wandered to the settee. "I think I will go for a short walk."

"Are you sure you are well enough?"

"Certainly," she replied firmly, "I have been lying about for days, and I am wild with restlessness. Do say that it is all right, Benny."

Mrs. Benjamin wavered.

"It is *your* salve that has really cured me, you know," Madeline added wickedly.

"Take a shawl."

Once her companion was gone, Madeline retrieved the letter she had received from beneath her pillow and read it again.

Dearest Madeline,

Things have been sadly flat here since you left Town. Fanny Prescott's come out was quite a sad crush. Sir George Wycoff has asked me several times as to your health. Poor man, he is quite concerned that you were suddenly so ill as to have to recuperate in the country! I was sorry I could not confide in him to allay his fears. But of course I did not, so rest assured on that head. He was kind enough to stand up with me at the Prescotts' ball and at Almack's. You will hate me to hear it, but I was given permission to waltz there by Lady Jersey herself only a week after you left. I hope you will not think me too disloyal if I admit that I was overjoyed. I am certain that you will be granted permission when you come back. After all, you had vouchers before the Incident!

As to the Incident itself, it was quite the talk for a few nights, but mostly people censored Lambrook. He has been seen courting Lord Dancy's mistress, and the rumor has it that when Dancy is back from France there will be quite a kickup over it. It is said that they hold gaming parties at her house every night. And it is the house Dancy set her up in. Of course, I don't know how much of this is true. My mama would have fits if she realized that I knew of any of this gossip!

Sir George has been simply heroic. He has tried to clear your name and has been ever so kind to me. I am sure that you must miss him terribly. I must close now, but know that I am thinking of you and I know that you will be back in Town soon.

Ever your friend,
Isabella

Postscript: I am going to Vauxhall with Sir George tomorrow night. I am sure that he would rather he was going with you!

Madeline laughed aloud. Sir George was really a very nice man, but it was so very obvious that he and Isabella would suit so much better than he and herself. Perhaps something good would come of her banishment after all.

Five

Feeling much improved once she was out of the house, Madeline wandered through the gardens and into the orchard. In London it would have been unheard of to go out unchaperoned, but here, solitude was the one luxury she realized that she had missed in the capital city. It was cool and dim under the shade of the trees, and the sun filtered though the leaves and dappled the walk with shifting shadows. The orchards had been neglected, since Aunt Enid thought them unfashionable and preferred to cultivate more exotic flora in the hothouse. There was several years' worth of leaves banking the trees, and the entire walk was permeated with the piquant, cidery smell of fermenting apples. It was a very calming place.

Madeline considered one of the tempting trees, branched often and low enough that they begged to be climbed, but the narrowness of her skirt and Mrs. Benjamin's imminent disapproval constrained her. Instead, she contented herself with seeing how far she could whack last year's fallen apples with her parasol. She was sadly noting that cider stained even cider-colored silk, when she heard footsteps crunching through the fallen leaves.

"You have caught me, Mr. Forth," she cried out when she saw that it was he. "You always seem to find me in the worst of situations. I assure you, I am not always in scrapes or acting bad-tempered."

"Surely it is only coincidence." He unbent enough to smile, and she made the objective observation that he was actually a little handsome. She was surprised that she had not noticed it before. Perhaps it was because he generally seemed so serious. Or cross.

"I have not seen you in several days. I trust that you have recovered from your fall?"

"Yes, sir. Thank you for your help." She watched him cautiously, unsure if he were still annoyed with her.

"Frederick misses you," he continued.

Madeline made a noise shockingly like a snort. "I doubt that."

"Of course he does. He exclaims every day on how happy he is that you are not around. A sure sign that he wishes very much you would return to the dancing lessons."

Madeline wondered briefly if Frederick was the only one who had missed her, but instantly chided herself for even thinking it. "Well, I shall go to see his fort this afternoon and shall play spillikins with him tonight. By then, we will have quarreled and things will be back to normal again." She laughed.

He smiled again, but did not laugh. "What are you doing here all alone, besides playing cricket with rotten apples?" he asked, and to her surprise, he fell into step beside her and they began walking companionably along the orchard walk.

"I am just amusing myself. It is very nice to be alone sometimes."

"Forgive me. I did not mean to disturb you."

"No, no, I did not mean that at all. I am delighted to see you outside of the torturous dancing parlor." She slanted a wicked glance at him. "Unless you plan to read me another sermon on propriety."

"I will try to restrain myself," he replied mildly. "Are you looking forward to the party?"

"Yes, I suppose. It will give me the chance to show off my newly acquired dancing skills."

"After only one lesson, I doubt I can claim any credit for your skills." He walked for a moment with his hands behind his back, obviously struggling with how to approach something. Madeline suddenly felt an unexpected flutter of nervousness. At last he began. "Miss Delaney, although your aunt appears to have no qualms about you appearing in public, I wonder if she is acting unwisely. Forgive me for speaking so plainly, but I am not sure that it would be appropriate for you to go to a social function, even here in the country, in . . . in your condition."

Madeline laughed. "Really, I am completely recovered. I am touched that you are concerned, but I do not think there is any cause to worry," she replied, giving a small skip and swinging her parasol to emphasize her words. Forth looked confused. "Are you coming to the party?" she asked politely.

"I do not think I will. Although Lady Hesstrow was kind enough to invite me. I think I might be out of place." He raised his chin in a defiant manner.

"I do not think you would be out of place. I wish you would go. Who knows what kind of hoydenish tricks I might try if you are not there to scowl at me?" she said in a teasing tone. "It will be on your head."

"I think not." He frowned. "You might be too intimidated to perform in front of your teacher."

"Me? Oh, I am hardly ever intimidated," she replied cheerfully.

"That I can believe." He actually laughed, and Madeline was pleased. They were silent for a moment, and she felt inexplicably tongue-tied. It was harder to converse with this man when he was being kind than when he was being horrid. She was aware that they had stopped walking and knew that she was standing entirely too close to him and gazing far too intently into his eyes. There was a painful silence, during which it seemed she could neither move nor breathe.

"You must miss the diversions of London," he said at last, visibly shrugging off the mood that had enveloped them. He resumed walking, and Madeline had no choice but to join him.

"Sometimes," she admitted, swinging her parasol with a little too much vigor. "Not quite so much as I'd thought. It is peculiar. I feel I spent my entire life getting ready for my season, and I only spent a few weeks in London doing season things and now"—she sighed—"now I look back and it all seems very silly and shallow. I mean, I did like all the dancing and attention and flowers and such, but it seemed as though there was a rule that you could only say a certain number of phrases to people.

"I think I only had real conversations with Isabella. And even they were not very philosophical," she mused. "They mostly concerned our beaux and dresses and rather . . . unimportant things like that. I suppose I had rather vague plans of marrying someone at some point. But at the time, it was pleasant to be admired and made much of. I never really thought of what my life would be like once the season was over. My fantasies of marrying the handsome foreign prince dissolved shortly after deciding what I would wear to the marriage ceremony."

She frowned. "I don't suppose I shall have any offers now, after what has happened. I suppose I shall be a spinster. Oh, dear. Perhaps I will become one of those crotchety old maids who keeps house for her father until the end of his days and then gets shuffled off as a companion to some relation. Good heavens, what if I have to play companion to Frederick's children or something awful like that? Not that Frederick is ever likely to marry, cheeky thing that he is. He replaced my perfume with vinegar, as though he thought I wouldn't notice, the little monsterling." She realized that she had been rambling and laughed aloud at herself. "No wonder you think me a featherwit."

He smiled at her with something akin to pity. "Perhaps things are not as bad as you think." They reached the end of the walk and turned back toward the house. "Perhaps you will meet someone in the country who does not pay a mind to Town gossip. After all, I am certain there are other girls in your . . . position."

Madeline sighed and whacked viciously with her parasol at a stand of tall grass. "I am not interested in marriage. My papa is obviously hoping I will make a brilliant marriage, but I want a love match."

"And your mother?"

"My mother died when I was very young."

"I am sorry."

"I did not know her." Madeline's tone indicated that she did not expect sympathy.

Forth again clasped his hands behind his back. "A love match," he repeated softly. "With Lambrook?"

"Lambrook?" Madeline was shocked. "No! That dreadful man?" She gave a disdainful laugh. "That was merely an indiscretion on my part."

Mr. Forth looked surprised. "It meant no more to you than it did to him?" His straight, dark brows drew together in a manner that she was beginning to associate with a forthcoming pompous lecture.

"Well, I would not say that," she said quickly.

"You were never in love with him?" It seemed as though he were annoyed that she had not been.

"Not a bit." She shrugged. "I just thought it would be a lark."

"A lark!" he exclaimed, working himself into an outrage worthy of her father. He looked at her intently, and his anger collapsed. "You have no idea of the magnitude of what you have done, have you?"

"Obviously, I do not," she replied, confused.

"You seem little more than a child." His tone conveyed disappointment, and he moved imperceptibly away from her.

"I will be nineteen in four months," she countered. "Girls of sixteen were presented with me this year." She drew her shawl closer. It was cooler in the shade than she had expected.

Forth shook his head. "Little wonder they are so foolish." He patted her arm in a consoling, pitying manner and sighed. Madeline was bewildered. What mood swings this man had! He seemed to take things so very seriously. Besides, her banishment to the country was no concern to him, so there was no need to act out a Cheltenham tragedy. Why could he not behave like the other men she knew in London? They were always polite and praised her extravagantly, and they never lectured her on propriety or looked at her with such pity. She did not speak to him on the way back to the house.

* * *

"Why don't you go out and join the fine folk in the dancing?" one of the housemaids asked, as Devin lounged in the doorway of the ballroom. "You can go in, you know. I heard that Lord Hesstrow invited you, what with you being in the family, after all."

Devin smiled thinly and shrugged. Unable to explain his reluctance to be a part of the festivities, he had told himself that he was merely curious to see how Madeline was getting on with her dancing. He had been extremely surprised that Lady Hesstrow was anxious to parade her niece when that young lady was known to be ruined in London. Perhaps the news had not followed her here. Certainly her family was hoping to marry her off to some country gentleman without his knowledge that she was damaged goods.

Again, he felt a surge of anger toward Lambrook. That man definitely knew the consequences of dallying with a young, unmarried woman, even if Madeline herself did not. Their conversation in the orchard had shocked him. Did she really hold her virtue so casually that she could shrug off her seduction? And what kind of cold woman could shrug off her lover as a mere indiscretion. Perhaps she had had a string of lovers. What trick was her family trying to pull by passing her off as an innocent and giving her a season on the marriage mart? It was an outrage!

Although Lady Hesstrow had invited nearly fifty couples, he saw Madeline immediately. She looked very much older in her ballgown of silver and white, and he was struck again by the realization that she was indeed a woman and not a girl. She turned as he watched her, and he knew that she saw him. He sensed in an instant that she must have seen the disapproval on his face, for her smile collapsed into an expression of hurt confusion. Then her chin went up and she turned from him to her partner and embarked on an animated discussion involving a good deal of laughter. She played the part of the innocent well, he thought, with a quiet noise of derision. It was a good thing that he was not involved.

Ensconced at her writing desk in her dressing gown after Mrs. Benjamin had left her, Madeline wrote:

Dearest Isabella,

I hope that you are well and enjoying the season. How was Vauxhall? I am so disappointed to have missed that outing. I was happy to hear that dear Fanny Prescott's come-out was a success. I am sure Frances Chandler will have stolen all of my beaux by this time, and you can tell her that she is welcome to them.

Here Madeline paused and recut her quill pen pensively, unsure of how to proceed. Then she continued slowly.

Elmhurst is tolerable. I had a fall from a horse shortly after I arrived and have spent most of my time recovering from that. Do not worry, it was a trifling incident. My cousin Frederick is insufferable, but I consent to amuse him as a good cousin should. You must see his marvelous fort! How I longed to be ten again!

Frederick's tutor is acting as my dancing master. This was a plot conceived by my aunt to have me partner him (Frederick) so that he may learn. It is very tedious, but because of my fall, we have only met once for dancing. The tutor is a dreadful, prosey man who is forever lecturing me on propriety. You, however, I am sure would find him romantic. He is the poor, disowned grandson of the Earl of Somerton, and he has a mysterious, penetrating look about him that I am sure you would instantly fall in love with. Not soulful like Lord Byron, but something else. Happily, he is not at all to my taste, for I find him detestably pompous.

My aunt has just thrown a party which was frightfully dull compared to those held in London. I was partnered in every dance and universally admired to a rather ridiculous extent, but the event seemed rather flat. I know it is bad-tempered and cross of me, but it seemed all the men were too old or too young or too silly, and possessed far less social address than those in London. It was not an unpleasant evening, but at the same time it was rather stifling, as I did not know any of the young people invited and felt rather on display by my aunt. (Uncle

Edgar pronounced me fine-looking and disappeared into the card room at the earliest opportunity.)

I felt most unlike myself. It must be that I have been so out of society of late, but I was positively nervous. And you know I am almost never nervous—even when we were presented at court. That horrid train! I shall never live down the humiliation of that day! Every time a new arrival was announced, I had to look up, hopeful that it would be someone interesting. But alas, there was no one of any interest whatsoever.

Do write to me, dear Isabella, for, as you can tell, I am languishing here in want of good company! I hope the Incident has not been bandied about too much. Perhaps if it has not, I may come home soon. It would be such a pity to miss the whole season. The idea of staying the summer here makes me absolutely distraught! I miss you terribly, and I hope you have not forgotten me in the midst of your social whirl. I want to hear about every minute of it!

Madeline closed the letter and sealed it. She felt slightly better, but still lay in bed for a very long time before she finally fell asleep.

Roderick Fennwick, duke of Lambrook muttered an exceedingly impolite phrase for the seventh time in as many minutes. "Well?" he inquired fiercely.

"Sorry, Your Grace, but the axle's broke." His

tiger looked up impassively from the wreck of the racing curricle.

"Can you fix it?" Lambrook snapped.

"Fix it?! Lord, no!" The tiger appeared slightly incredulous at his employer's lack of knowledge. "Ye took that turn too tight," he offered. Lambrook quelled any further commentary with a dire look.

He cursed himself for setting off from London in only the curricle and not leaving for his ancestral seat with his baggage and servants in his traveling coach. He cursed Lord Dancy and his possessive ways. He cursed the curricle and the tiger, and then instructed the latter to stay with the former and started off on foot to find help. It was thus that he came to be found, three-quarters of an hour later, in the drawing room of Elmhurst.

"Good heavens! What good fortune that you were not killed in the accident!" Lady Hesstrow exclaimed, for perhaps the fourth time. "However, we here at Elmhurst must consider ourselves fortunate and shall profit by your accident by keeping you here for a visit until your vehicle is repaired."

"Madam, I should be charmed to spend some time at your most elegantly appointed estate." He smiled, showing his even, extremely white teeth.

"Oh, well, Your Grace, we shall ensure that you have excellent company. We hope you shall not lack for London amusements here. In fact, I was just saying to my husband the other day that it would be lovely if we were to have a modest dinner party. We often entertain. In fact, Lord Hesstrow is a close personal friend of Lord Taunton and we often have the Winthrop family out for hunting parties. The Stantons, Lady William Stanton is great niece to Lord Brougham himself, you know, visit us every year on their way from Town to their own country estate. Of course, it shall not be so elaborate as you are used to. We are sadly provincial here, but we shall endeavor!

"In fact, my young niece is here from London," Lady Hesstrow continued without a pause. "She started her season, but, alas, her health is like mine, a delicate flower. The stresses of the season were too much for her, and she is recovering from exhaustion with us. Thankfully my family has a collection of remedies which are quite remarkable. Her recovery has been nothing short of miraculous, and I must say that I believe it is entirely due to my famous tisanes. Of course, her companion, a dragon of a woman, will keep interfering and dosing the poor creature with her own poisonous concoctions, but I believe we will cure the dear girl in spite of it.

"She is barely out of the schoolroom, but I am sure that she will be head over ears to meet someone with a little Town bronze, as they say." Lambrook merely nodded and gave her a bland smile. His eyes drifted disinterestedly around the room. "Williams," called Lady Hesstrow in her best lady-of-the-house tone, "send for Miss Delaney to come and meet our visitor."

Six

When Madeline entered the room, Lambrook's eyes boldly perused her body and passed over her face without the slightest hint of recognition. Her own reaction was somewhat more pronounced. She felt her first fiery blush give way to a blanch that took her to near fainting. This could not possibly be happening! But there was no doubt that it was Lambrook. He was not the kind of man one would forget. His height and broad shoulders made him tower over most people. His face was conventionally handsome, but with black brows seemingly perpetually set at a sarcastic angle, and there was a peculiar harshness to his features.

Madeline swayed on her feet for a moment and was entirely unable to speak, but Lady Hesstrow was mercifully oblivious of her change in demeanor. "This is my dear niece Miss Madeline Delaney, Your Grace. Madeline, the Duke of Lambrook was traveling to his estate, but he had the most frightful carriage accident down the road. He will be staying with us until the repairs are made."

Lambrook spoke first. "Miss Delaney, I am delighted to make your acquaintance." He smiled and bowed. As Madeline only made a faint gurgle in reply, he continued. "Your aunt has been telling me you made your bow this season, but were forced to leave Town early on account of illness. I am sorry we did not have a chance to meet under more fortuitous circumstances. We must rectify that omission."

She stared. Was it possible that he was saying this without irony? His face was impassive, with only the slightest hint of a leer on it. It was almost the same look he had presented to her when he had met her for the first time. Did he not recognize her? Noting that her aunt was staring very hard at her because of her lack of response to this charming introduction, she managed to stammer her delight at the meeting. She marveled that she could ever have found him attractive. Even Mr. Forth was more attractive. His chin was strong, where Lambrook's was weak. The chiseled lines of Lambrook's face, which she had previously thought of as piratical, she now saw as signs of dissipation.

Lady Hesstrow had launched into an account of Madeline's own accident, which was vastly improved by the addition of several harrowing details which had not occurred in the original misadventure. Mr. Forth, whom prior to the incident she had rarely directly acknowledged as a relation, played a prominent role in the recounted tale. After a few more minutes of conversation, during which Lambrook still showed no recognition, Madeline was allowed to retire, still puzzling.

"I should like to call him out myself!" she announced dramatically to Mrs. Benjamin, slamming the door of her room. "I shall have Uncle toss him out of the house with a flea in his ear!" She grimaced maliciously and began brushing her hair with unnecessary vigor.

"What are you going on about, pet?" her duenna asked in alarm.

"Lambrook." Madeline spat out the word.

"The man who—"

"The man from the Mealington-Smythe ball. The man who ruined me." She brandished the brush at her own reflection.

The older woman's brows rose in alarm. "At this house!"

"It is quite all right, Benny," Madeline continued with some asperity. "He did not recognize me."

"Stop it now; you will pull it all out." Mrs. Benjamin extracted the brush from her charge's hand and began to comb through Madeline's hair herself. She clicked her tongue to her teeth for quite a while before continuing. "Perhaps he genuinely does not recognize you. You have gotten rather pale, my dear. I suspect it is those infernal tisanes!" She made a visible effort to control her wrath. "Or perhaps he has no desire to stir up anything and make a scene. Unless we want to make a scene ourselves and have him ejected from the house, we must play dumb and continue the charade. We shall forget the entire thing, and he shall be gone in a few days." She shook her head. "Not as though I wouldn't like to throttle him myself."

Madeline only made a murderous noise under her breath. "We will just put the best face on things," Mrs. Benjamin continued firmly, "and you shall stay out of his way." She cocked a stern eye at the girl.

Madeline laughed, but the sound was harsh. "No, Benny, you needn't worry on my account. I can see Lord Lambrook for what he is now, and I am not about to be taken in by his charms a second time. I may be a fool, but I am not stupid." She examined herself in the mirror and found that the grim line of her lips and the fierce sparkle of her eyes were more frightening than becoming, so she spent a few moments smoothing her features into more placid lines. Her companion helped her into her most demure dress. It was a rather dowdy affair of pearl gray trimmed with forest green ribbons, but Madeline hoped to remain unnoticed.

"Ah, Mr. Forth, you have arrived. Now we are all here. I hope that you don't mind if we dine *en famille,* Your Grace. This is my sister's nephew, Mr. Devin Forth. I told you about how he rescued dear Madeline from certain death on that wild horse." Lady Hesstrow gestured graciously at the tutor.

Madeline had recovered enough from the shock of seeing Lambrook at Elmhurst to be interested in Mr. Forth's reaction to his unexpected presence. Forth looked taken aback for only a moment and then bowed in acknowledgment to Lambrook's greeting. It was unsurprising that Lambrook should not recognize him, as they had only been in each other's presence a few minutes and he himself had been quite the worse for wear at the time.

Devin's eyes flickered to hers in alarm. She could only raise her shoulders slightly in an expression of helpless bewilderment before Lady Hesstrow was shepherding her over to take Lord Hesstrow's arm while she herself took Lambrook's in the grand procession in to dinner. Madeline watched his back with loathing. How dare he invade her sanctuary? Was there no end to the humiliation she was to suffer because of him? She wondered vaguely how she would ever manage to unclench her teeth in order to eat.

"There now, Lord Lambrook. You will sit down at my right. And Madeline dear, next to him. Are you quite all right Madeline? I declare you look quite flushed. Shall I have one of my family's well-known—"

"I am quite well, Aunt." Madeline cut her off, seeing Mrs. Benjamin begin to swell. Mr. Forth was seated on her other side. She had hoped to gain some comfort from his presence, but his brows were set in a belligerent line. He was watching her closely, but he returned her weak smile with a censorious scowl.

"How did you manage to get him here?" he demanded in an undertone.

"I didn't," she hissed. How like the man to assume she had somehow managed to engineer this disaster.

Lambrook looked benignly around the table. "How gracious of you to accommodate me, Lord Hesstrow. I shall never recover from the embarrassment of having descended upon you without an invitation."

Hesstrow bobbed his head and applied himself to the soup.

His wife beamed. "We are delighted to have this wonderful chance to become more acquainted with you. How nice it is to meet people who have interests like one's own. I daresay our families will become fast friends because of this happy accident. Of course, if we had known you were coming we would have planned something special for our dinner. I am positively ready to sink with shame that we shall have only four removes. I declare you will think we are positively provincial. But I do hope you will try the pigeon pie. Elmhurst is quite famous for its pigeon pie. Why, nearly a century ago dear Edmund's ancestors were known for dishing out delicious pigeon pie. Our chef is counted one of the best in the county. He is French, of course."

"Saw your horses," Lord Hesstrow volunteered

unexpectedly. "Touched in the wind, both of them. I hope you didn't pay too much for them, sir. They're fine lookers, but I doubt they'll keep their paces longer than a year."

Lambrook's faint scowl at Lord Hesstrow's comment passed fleetingly. "Ah, well, I won them in a game of hazard. I could hardly turn them down when the man thought himself quite daring to have wagered them in the first place." He gave a nonchalant wave of his hand. He turned to Madeline and asked softly, "Do you think me very reckless?"

"Yes," she replied to her plate.

"Do you think I will break my neck with recklessness?" He gave her a teasing glance.

Madeline was tempted to reply that she very much hoped so. "When will your carriage be repaired?" she asked coolly.

"Do you wish to be rid of me?" he chided gently.

"Miss Delaney, Frederick desired me to ask if you would come up to the schoolroom tomorrow after lessons. He is in possession of a rather large frog he would very much like you to see," Mr. Forth interrupted in a grave voice.

"How flattering that I am counted an expert. I suspect if I were to decline the invitation, I would end up with the specimen in my bed."

"I would hope Frederick has more manners than that."

"But you know he does not." She laughed.

"He's not half as devious as some children,"

Devin replied pointedly, leaving no doubt that she was the child he had in mind.

"Oh, London nearly killed poor Madeline, did it not, my dear?" Lady Hesstrow called down from the head of the table.

"I was a little tired from the season," she managed to choke out, her fingers itching to strangle the man who sat placidly beside her. Actually, she could happily have strangled either man who sat beside her.

"How did you find the city otherwise?" Lambrook asked politely.

"Oh, I like it very well. I have lived there a good portion of every year since I was a child."

"Indeed, as I have myself. How magnificent that we would at last meet, and in Somerset of all places."

"How very bizarre," she said dryly.

Mr. Forth cleared his throat. "Did Lord Hesstrow find another mount for you? I am not certain your mare is at all suitable. I spoke with him about it, and he said he would provide a tamer animal."

"How very kind."

"Yes, I should hate—that is, we should all hate— for an accident to befall you. Because of your imprudence," he added.

Madeline shot him a look of frustration and lapsed into silence, feeling very trapped between her dinner partners.

After countless painfully long courses, during which only Lady Hesstrow and Lambrook made any attempts at conversation, the ladies left the men to their port and adjourned to the parlor. Judging from the extremely speaking looks that her aunt had been sending her way all evening, Madeline knew she was in for a lecture. She slipped quickly to the pianoforte and began one of the few minuets she played with any proficiency, but was adroitly followed to the instrument by Lady Hesstrow, who looked vaguely like a puce-colored thundercloud in her overly trimmed gown.

"Madeline!" she hissed, as though the gentlemen could possibly overhear her from their seats in the dining room down the hall. "How could you be so rude to our distinguished guest? I would have thought you had more manners than that! He is a very handsome and influential man from London, and you are snubbing him! With manners like that, it is little wonder you didn't take!"

Despite the inaccuracy of the remark, Madeline flushed. She took a moment to recover herself. "But, Aunt Enid, I was only trying to save you embarrassment. You see, in Town, Lord Lambrook is not received." She said this with apparent worry and innocence, and was rewarded to see Lady Hesstrow's face go red in her turn.

"Not received?" she repeated vaguely.

"Oh, no. His reputation is quite awful. The best families cut him entirely. However, there is nothing to be done now, since you cannot possibly ask him to leave."

"Not received . . ." Lady Hesstrow repeated

again. "Oh, dear. What shall we do? I shall have Edmund make him leave. Oh, dear, you should have said . . . Oh . . . I must go lie down. I feel very unwell. Please make my excuses to everyone. . . ." Slightly wild-eyed, she fled the room.

The men entered the parlor soon afterward and Madeline excused her aunt's sudden indisposal. She then sat sewing, determinedly keeping her eyes down and answering only in monosyllables. If she stabbed the linen with too much vigor, no one commented upon it. At last, after several strained hours, she announced her intention to go to bed. Lord Lambrook escorted her to the door of the room. "I am sorry not to have had the opportunity to have spoken more with you, Miss Delaney," he purred. Madeline inadvertently pulled back from him, repulsed.

"I hope you have a pleasant stay here," she replied woodenly, knowing that her remark did not address his comment. "Good night," she added firmly and retreated hastily upstairs.

Madeline sat in the deep windowsill of the second-best drawing room with a book that she was not reading. She started when Mr. Forth entered the room and scowled when she felt a guilty flush rise up her neck.

"Miss Delaney, you are early," he remarked pleasantly enough. "I thought Mrs. Benjamin said three o'clock for the dancing lessons. How are you today?" He did not allude to their verbal sparring of the night before.

"I am well, Mr. Forth," she replied coolly.

He sat down beside her and picked up the piece of green velvet ribbon that had fallen to the floor. "What is this?"

"It is a bookmark," she replied. There was a rather long moment of silence, during which Madeline pretended to read. She turned several pages, but was far too aware of the man beside her to digest any information.

"You did not appear to be enjoying yourself last night," he said at last.

"I was not," she agreed tersely. She opened her mouth to explain, but stopped herself. They sat for another painful moment in silence, Mr. Forth twining the ribbon around his fingers and Madeline staring at a line of print. "You see," she began with a sigh, "I am extremely displeased that Lambrook is here."

"I recall your last meeting." His voice was still quiet, but had a dangerous edge.

"Yes, that was not at all pleasant."

"Has he changed his mind?" he asked, his jaw tight.

"Changed his mind? About what?"

"Offering for you."

"Proposing?" Madeline laughed bitterly. "He does not remember who I am."

"He did not come here to find you to make an offer?" The man had the audacity to appear almost pleased.

"No, he did not," she shot back, wounded. "And I would not accept him if he made one." She paused a moment, thinking. "Do you think, Mr. Forth, that you could do me a favor?"

"I will do anything you wish," he replied.

"I have a plan, you see." She smiled beguilingly. "Could you, perhaps, pretend to be a bit partial to me over the next few days—just so that Lord Lambrook doesn't . . . bother me?" She opened her eyes wide, in a pleading expression.

For a moment he gazed into her face and appeared to be ready to agree. Then the meaning of her words seemed to sink in and his expression immediately became shuttered. "You want to use me to make Lord Lambrook jealous?"

"Well, I"—Madeline dropped her eyes and felt her face grow hot—"I know it sounds foolish . . . but—"

"It is foolish," he said bluntly.

"Mr. Forth!" It was almost the wail of a spoiled child.

"Miss Delaney," he began firmly, taking her by the arms as though he longed to shake her, "I know very little about Lord Lambrook, or your former dealings with him, but it is not fitting for you to make a cake of yourself by playing childish games to try to manipulate him into falling in love with you. That is more suited to one of your silly gothic novels." He gestured to the book in her hand. "Lambrook should have done the right thing by you and married you. However, I am convinced that would not have brought you happiness. Did you not hear anything the cad said outside his club? He cares nothing for you. Despite what society may think, you are better off starting a new life without him. You are better off here, even in the state you are in, amongst family."

Madeline turned on him with a fierceness that startled him. "Yes, you know little about Lord Lambrook," she hissed, flinging her book to the floor and standing over him. "He is not a gentleman. You saw only the horribly, humiliating end of the fiasco! Lord Lambrook is the reason I am rusticating in this horrid place with my reputation in shreds."

"I gathered that," Forth replied soothingly, attempting to placate her.

"Lord Lambrook compromised my reputation, and the man does not even recognize me!" She began pacing during this speech and delivered this last line with the fury of a Drury Lane tragedienne. Mr. Forth looked as though he half-expected her to fling herself on the floor, gnashing her teeth. She did not. Instead she stood in front of him, breathless, her face flushed and her eyes blazing. He stood and put his hands on her shoulders to calm her, his hands moving slowly up and down her arms in an unconscious caress.

Madeline's anger suddenly surged into desire, but she was so surprised by this she could not react. Forth, suddenly seeming to realize that he was touching her, pulled away. He calmly offered her his handkerchief even though she was not crying, and urged her to sit again.

"Miss Delaney, I am sorry to have overset you. It was wrong of me to speak so familiarly to you. I should not have mentioned the events of that day." He almost patted her arm, but seemed to think better of it.

"I am ruined—I will never be received—and Lambrook wouldn't offer for me and I missed my first season." She found, to her annoyance that she sounded pathetically close to tears after all.

"Are you with child?" Devin asked bluntly.

She turned on him in horror. "What? No!" The self-pity instantly evaporated and the raging harridan was back. "How dare you say that! It was nothing like that. I waltzed with him before I was given permission at Almack's, and he took me alone out in the garden and kissed me. I didn't even like it!" she cried. "I am not a lightskirt! We did not have any secret assignations!"

Devin Forth laughed. He was the only man who knew about that humiliating day. He was the only one she could talk to, but when she bared her heart to him, he laughed. First, he insulted her by thinking that she had actually done . . . that— and with Lambrook of all people! And then he laughed at her! And it was loud and unrestrained, and he sounded relieved.

"He only kissed you in the garden?"

"And waltzed with me," Madeline reminded him sharply.

"You silly goose! And all this time I thought . . ." He laughed again, ignoring her furious expression. "Only a kiss? My dear girl, if that was all, you are hardly alone with your 'shredded reputation'!"

Madeline glared at him, unable to speak. She didn't know if she was more shocked at his assumption of her wantonness or embarrassed at her obvious naïveté.

"Well, if you do not think it was such a horrible thing, why am I here?" she demanded.

"I suspect your father was upset that the incident happened, especially when it probably did cause some talk and the man did not offer for you or appear to hold any feeling for you." He glanced briefly at Madeline's murderous expression. "Furthermore, the incident involved a man of such a dubious reputation that he decided it would keep you out of harm's and scandal's way to have you go for a short, recuperative trip to the country."

He laughed again. Until this conversation, Madeline had hardly ever even seen him smile, not to mention such prolonged fits of hilarity. Considering he was laughing at her expense, it was not very flattering.

"I suspect if your father knew that Lambrook was here, he would ship you right back to London." He put his finger under her chin and forced her to look at him. He then smiled at her encouragingly until she at last managed a thin smile in return. When he dropped her chin, she felt slightly deflated.

"So you will help me?" she asked at last, standing up and wandering away from him.

"On what account?" He was still looking extremely amused about his misunderstanding of her relationship with Lambrook.

"On Lord Lambrook's!" she replied in exasperation. "What shall I do about him?"

"I would suggest that you do nothing," he replied, absently putting her ribbon bookmark into his waistcoat pocket.

"Nothing?"

"Yes, no revenge, no speeches, no poisoning, no making him jealous, no making him sorry. If, as you say, he does not recognize you, you may simply be polite and hope that his stay is not protracted. Your aunt is unlikely to want to broadcast his presence here, now that she knows he is not received." There was a wicked glint in his gray eyes.

"How do you know——?"

"Frederick told me that you told Lady Hesstrow." He laughed. "The schoolroom grapevine."

"So you think I should just do . . . nothing?" Madeline collapsed into her seat again and looked forlorn. She looked strange there—a bizarre chimera of child and woman. Her hands knotted the ribbons of her dress in a childish expression of anxiety, while the light shone on the smooth part of her hair, relieved from severity by a cluster of curls at the crown. The honey brown looked more gold than otherwise in the late afternoon sun. She would have been quite beautiful if not for her comic grimace at being deprived of wreaking vengeance on Lord Lambrook.

"I am afraid so," he replied solemnly. "Unfortunately, as a lady of good breeding, you are encouraged to be tolerant and not to scheme and create convoluted plots of revenge that are bound to go awry as in a bad play." She had sat down beside him on the deep windowsill, but now it was he who shifted uncomfortably and moved across the room, absently straightening pictures and thumbing through sheet music.

"How awful! How . . . dull!" Madeline leaned her head on her fist in an attitude of despondency. "I can't imagine going my whole life being proper and stodgy." She glanced at him out of the corner of her eye. "Like you," she added.

"Like me," Forth repeated with a sigh. "I suppose I should call Lambrook out like an honorable, romantic hero, but instead I am the voice of reason." His look was paternal, and Madeline became annoyed again.

"I suppose you are right." She stood and lifted her shoulders in a half-shrug. "Here is your handkerchief," she said in a flat voice, holding out the rather bland, utilitarian cloth to him. There was a moment of silence before he took it.

"You left in the middle of your first season," he said suddenly.

"Yes."

"That must have been very difficult for you." He paused for a moment. "Is it so very terrible here?" His voice was unexpectedly gentle and low.

Madeline felt her heart twitch in a peculiar way and suddenly became slightly nervous. He stood much closer to her now than people usually did during the course of a conversation. She longed for him to touch her, but he only looked searchingly into her eyes. She suspected they betrayed her, revealing fear mingled with adoration, or perhaps something even more embarrassing. In order to put the conversation back into less frightening territory she assumed an air of arch coquettishness. "Oh, no. It is quite pleasant here, now that I have you to amuse me," she replied with a sly glance and a pert smile. She instantly regretted what she had done; the moment was lost. Forth stood up with a grim smile.

"Yes, I suppose I am an amusement for you," he returned evenly, his face once again assuming the familiar mask of disapproval. Madeline longed to grab him by the coat sleeve and plead that she had not meant what she had said. She did not, and he went on. "Although, Miss Delaney, I am pleased that you have not ruined yourself in the true sense, I think it would be best to remind you that all of this probably came about because of your behavior. I hope you will mend your reckless, thoughtless ways before you end up with more trouble than a slightly tarnished reputation." And looking as if he had never laughed in his life, he turned to greet Mrs.

Benjamin and Frederick, who had arrived for the dancing lesson.

It was only at Lord Hesstrow's insistence that Enid did not retreat behind the veil of hypochondria and hide entirely from her unwelcome guest. Tonight, Madeline behaved better and managed to direct several barbless, tepid responses to Lord Lambrook's remarks. He continued to be superlatively pleasant, exhibiting his natural abundance of charm and grace, and he seemed intent on keeping Madeline engaged in conversation. Mr. Forth, who had hardly spoken to her during the course of the dancing lesson, did not direct any comments in her direction.

Madeline reminded herself over and over of that humiliating day, little more than a month ago, when Lambrook had rejected her so cruelly. She gripped the table leg under the cloth to keep from scratching his eyes out. Only the thought that she should soon have her revenge kept her taut smile from turning into a snarl. After dinner, the gentlemen did not linger long and soon joined the ladies.

"I hear, Miss Delaney, that you play and sing very well. Will you not honor us?" Lord Lambrook's smile seemed to show too many of his white teeth. She did not see how she could ever have found him attractive.

"I am afraid you have been misinformed," she replied coolly, but sat down and began to play.

She performed passably, though with no inflection, and did not merit the lavish praise that Lambrook offered. He begged for an encore and then stood beside her as she played in order to turn the pages. Madeline tolerated this with her teeth on edge. He seemed so odiously forward! His charm was so obvious and contrived. How could she ever have let him near her? She could have been married to him! This distressing thought made her lose her place, and she was forced to blushingly apologize and start again.

Her audience was not able to endure much of her lackluster playing, so Lord Hesstrow suggested whist. Lambrook submitted to this tame pastime without a murmur, though his enthusiasm for the game diminished when Madeline announced that she did not wish to play. She begged Mrs. Benjamin to take her place to make up the foursome and professed an ardent desire to work on her embroidery. Mrs. Benjamin, who knew how much she hated needlework, raised a cynical eyebrow. Mr. Forth also excluded himself. He sat at a silkwood writing desk, half-turned from her while he wrote a letter. Though she watched him for a long time, he neither paused nor looked up. His focused expression of concentration was much more flattering than the disapproving scowl she usually saw. If, perhaps, he had someone else's personality, she might be very attracted to him indeed.

For a long time, there was no sound in the room but the shifting of the curtains in the breeze from the open windows and the snap of the cards on the baize table. At last, Forth finished his correspondences and drifted over to where she sat in the pool of light from the lamp, staring out in thought, with her needlework in her lap. "You are doing very well," he said, careful that the whist players did not hear him.

"Am I not?" Madeline was pleased that he had noticed, but for the first time, began to doubt the propriety of her newest scheme. Dash the man! He only had to look at her and she was feeling guilty about improper conduct.

"You are doing the right thing to ignore him. Impeccable good breeding." He paused for a moment. "He is a snake, though."

"Isn't he? I cannot think what possessed me to fall prey to his charms as I did."

"I am having second thoughts about not calling him out."

"Why, Mr. Forth, you are a romantic after all!" Madeline laughed.

"You misjudge me entirely." He appeared entirely serious. "Causing his pride a fall would give me great pleasure entirely independent of defending your honor."

"Oh, dear, how unchivalrous," she commented vaguely, thinking about her honor. "What I did . . . it wasn't so very bad, was it? I mean, what happened in London, that . . . kissing incident. . . ." She willed the foolish blush to leave her cheeks.

"No, I assure you. I can see no reason for you

not to return to London at the end of the season. In fact, it might have been wiser for your father to have allowed you to stay and let the matter blow over. Reputations can withstand a few kisses." The words were kind, but his expression was unexpectedly dark. "I am surprised that you had not found this out before," he added in a slightly more acidic tone.

Madeline chose to ignore his remark. "Well, I am relieved. I would enjoy going back to London, but I am not sure how much I would enjoy the people. Looking back on them, they were terribly alike. And we always talked about the same things. I think I would have grown tired of it."

"Very likely," he replied, "However, I am sure you will find something in Town to divert you."

"Yes," Madeline said slowly, and then sat for a moment in thought. "Mr. Forth," she began suddenly in another tone, "I do hope you are not cross with me after our conversation in the drawing room."

"Why should I be?"

"All my plotting was very foolish. I do tend to be too managing sometimes." She looked up at him wheedlingly, feeling as though she were apologizing in advance for what was about to happen.

"I know, Miss Delaney. I had only forgotten for a moment that in some ways you are still a child."

"I am not!" she replied, with such heat that the players at the whist table looked over in some surprise, and she was forced to begin sewing with fierce industry.

"I know. But I think it would be best for me to continue to think of you as such." He wore a peculiar, grim-lipped expression as he left her side and went over to gather his papers together.

Seven

Madeline awoke when she heard the sounds of loud voices in the hallway. Slipping on her robe, she suppressed feelings of guilt. So the trap had been sprung. Well, it was hardly going to harm him, and he did bring it upon himself, she reminded herself.

"What the blazes are you doing out here making such a racket?" Lord Hesstrow was demanding as she stepped out into the hall.

In the hallway, wearing only a nightshirt, Lambrook was still shoving his shoulder against his bedroom door. "I have been locked out of my room," he replied nastily, his face a dull red as he surveyed the small crowd that had gathered.

"And what were you doing wandering around my house in the dead of the night?"

"Nothing," Lambrook snapped and then swore at the locked door in a voice audible enough to make Lady Hesstrow gasp.

"Been for a visit to Lizzy the upper chambermaid, I'll wager," an anonymous footman who had arrived at the scene remarked in an undertone. "I heard her saying that they was to meet."

Lady Hesstrow gasped again.

"I will not stand for this sort of conduct," Lord Hesstrow boomed. "This is my house, and I am responsible for my servants. I will thank you for behaving in a manner suitable to a guest for the remainder of your stay." Hesstrow eyed him coldly. "I suggest that we all return to bed and forget this incident."

"But I can't get into my demmed room!" Lambrook protested, throwing himself again against the door.

"How did you manage to lock yourself out?" Lady Hesstrow chided.

"I don't know. The door is jammed. Someone contrived to lock me out."

"Good heavens, what nonsense! Is there anyone in your room who could have locked you out? Your valet?" Enid suggested.

"Didn't bring a valet." Lord Hesstrow reminded his wife. "Is Lizzy in there?" he demanded suspiciously.

"No. For God's sake, just let me into my room!"

"I'll break down the door," the footman volunteered eagerly.

Madeline left and went back into her own bedroom without waiting to see the end of the scene. She was happy that Mr. Forth had not been present, for he surely would have seen in her expression that she was responsible for this. But really, she reminded herself, if Lambrook had not left his room for a midnight assignation, this would not have happened. If he was going to carry on in such a manner while he was a guest in the house, he deserved to be humiliated. She did not feel very much better.

It would have been nice if she could have blamed Frederick, but he had only provided the technical expertise, while she had conceived the plan. He would be delighted to know that his device had worked. Lambrook had gone to his bedroom when everyone had retired for the night. He obviously, as Frederick and Madeline had hoped, had not noticed that his door was closed but not latched. Frederick's method of jamming the lock's tumblers had allowed the door to be opened from the inside, but not from the outside once it was closed. If Lambrook was so indiscreet as to leave his room in the middle of the night, he would be trapped outside.

Madeline burrowed deeper under the covers. She was neither surprised nor hurt that Lambrook was seducing the serving girls. She would have been more surprised to learn that he had not been. Forth would not approve, but she did feel a modicum better knowing that she was not the only one who knew this man to be less than the paragon he pretended to be. Perhaps now her uncle would encourage him to leave the house. Well, whether he did or not, she hoped that Mr. Forth would not connect the events of this night with her.

* * *

"Well, pet, how was your ride?"

"Very good, Benny." Madeline unpinned her riding hat and flung it onto the dressing table. "Hendrikson the groom is helping me improve my horsemanship."

"Did you fall off?" Mrs. Benjamin asked cheerfully.

"No, I did not."

"Well, I do think your uncle could have provided you with a more gentle horse after that wild one threw you."

"Uncle felt that it would be better for me to learn on Daisy, so I would not be frightened of her. Actually she has turned out to be the sweetest creature imaginable. She only spooks at loud noises. I never worry about being thrown now." She poured some water into the basin and began washing her face.

"Your aunt is quite upset after last night," Mrs. Benjamin commented as she helped her change into a canary yellow- and white-striped morning gown.

"I am not surprised. First finding out that he is not received and now the evidence as to why. I feel quite sorry for her."

"Indeed she is quite prostrate. Perhaps I should send up a posset to her. . . ." Mrs. Benjamin's eyes gleamed wickedly.

"Will they ask him to leave?"

"I don't see how they can; he is their guest you know. One would think he would understand that he is no longer welcome. Seducing the servants!

Oh! If your aunt only knew the half of it!" her duenna exclaimed fiercely. "He has some nerve!" Her voice was comically at odds with the careful and deliberate manner in which she put the finishing touches on the yellow ribbons tying up Madeline's hair.

"Well, I for one am hardly surprised. We should forget the whole incident." She ignored Mrs. Benjamin's look of surprise at her lack of vitriol, and went downstairs. She was relieved to find that Lady Hesstrow was the only occupant of the breakfast room.

"Oh, Madeline my dear. Whatever shall we do?"

"What can we do, ma'am? He must be asked to leave."

Lady Hesstrow looked stricken. "But he is a duke! You cannot ask a duke to leave! Though I hear everything in his dukedom that was not entailed has been gambled away. . . ." She took a minuscule bite of toast and chewed it thoughtfully. "But really, Hesstrow should not tolerate his behavior. And if he is not received in London—"

"We cannot be expected to receive him here," Madeline finished for her.

"Indeed. But I had such high hopes of our acquaintance with him! I have already sent out invitations for a Venetian breakfast! Oh, dear, whatever am I going to do about that? He was to be the guest of honor. I had also engaged the musicians for a moonlit ridotto. This is terrible indeed." She sat for a long moment in silence, pondering this calamity.

"It is very strange how the door managed to become stuck shut as it did. It took nearly an hour for a footman to disengage the lock on the door. It would serve Lambrook right if he caught a cold standing out in the corridor in his nightshirt for all that time. It's shocking, really!"

"He must be asked to go," Madeline repeated.

"But what if he did catch cold and we were to throw him out and then everyone should say such terrible things about us. A duke!" she wailed. "If only he were a viscount. I could have had Edmund throw out a viscount. Perhaps even an earl, but it would have to have been something quite reprehensible. A murder or some such thing. Really, the man is a peer, after all. No, I do not believe we can ask him to leave."

Madeline frowned. "But think of poor Lizzy!"

"Oh, the girl's a strumpet anyway."

Her niece conceded defeat. "I think I shall go sketch in the garden."

"Yes, I do believe if we can keep this matter quiet we may still have the breakfast and perhaps even the ridotto as well. Perhaps people in Town will say that we are a dashing fast set, but really, I don't believe we care a rush what people think of us." Her aunt looked quite delighted.

Madeline rose to leave.

"Yes, a dashing fast set indeed . . ." Her aunt sat pondering the implications of her new reputation.

Madeline fled the room just as Mr. Forth entered. He bowed as she darted past him, but she ducked her head to avoid his eyes. She heard him calmly ask her aunt her opinion about Frederick's progress in Latin.

Knowing that he was safely out of the way, Madeline dashed up the stairs to the schoolroom. Frederick was there, minutely examining the inner workings of a disemboweled mantel clock.

"Did it work?" he asked

"Yes, rather too well. Lambrook was stuck outside in the corridor for an hour while a footman tried to unjam the door." She stood in the doorway, looking anxiously down the hall for signs of the returning tutor.

"I told you I was good at inventing things," her cousin remarked with a profound lack of modesty. He shook the clock and several more pieces fell out.

"Well, Freddie, I want to thank you for your help and to ask you not to mention it to anyone."

"Of course not!" He looked offended that she would question his discretion.

"Particularly Mr. Forth," she added.

"Oh," he said mildly, "I already told him."

"What? Oh, Freddie, how could you?" she began, but she was stopped by the sound of someone mounting the stairs. "Was he angry?" she hissed.

"Not with me. He said that I was clever."

"I mean with me!"

Frederick paused and smugly appeared to think for several maddening seconds while she wavered at the doorway, poised for flight. "Yes," he replied at last. Madeline only shot him a look promising awesome retribution and escaped down the hall. He was calmly beginning to reinsert pieces of the clock back into its casing when Mr. Forth entered the schoolroom.

"Was that Madeline?" he asked.

"Yes. She ran away when she heard you coming." Frederick kicked his heels against the rungs of his chair and continued his work without offering any more information.

"Why?" Devin prompted at last.

"I suppose she was afraid because you are angry with her. About the door I mean."

"Well, it was very foolish of her," Mr. Forth announced. He shoved his fists into his pockets and crossed the room to stare out the window with an annoyed expression.

"Yes," Frederick agreed cheerfully. "Perhaps we should lock her out of her room to show her how it feels."

"I don't think so. Miss Delaney is a young lady now, even though she does not always act like one. She is entirely out of my jurisdiction." He saw a small figure dressed in yellow cross from the house into the garden and turned, scowling, from the window.

"What does jurisdiction mean?"

"Stop kicking your chair, Frederick," Forth snapped, then continued more kindly, "it means that she is not my charge, like you are."

"Well, you pay a lot of attention to her." The boy's tone was almost accusing. "You are often watching her when you think no one is looking and—"

"That is outside of enough, Frederick," his tutor interrupted. "Let us talk instead of geography." His voice was stern, but he ran a hand through his hair in an unconscious gesture of frustration.

Madeline reached the garden, still stalking with unladylike strides and muttering under her breath. Her guilt conveniently replaced by annoyance, she cursed the interfering Mr. Forth and his nasty, judgmental ways. However, she did not have the stamina to remain irate for very long, as the May sun was high and the unseasonably warm, heavy air was still and cloyingly sweet with fragrance. Her steps slowed lethargically as the heat evaporated her irritation, and she dropped at last onto a stone bench. It was still cool from the morning and shaded by a net of shadows cast from the rose trellis.

For a long time she simply sat and watched the tiny bugs swirl dizzily above the flower beds, wondering how they managed to keep up their energy. Finally, she settled down to draw a portion of the wall where wisteria grew unpruned. She had made a rather indifferent start, when suddenly the page was darkened by a shadow. She looked up, her heart leaping, and saw with some disappointment that it was Lord Lambrook.

"What a talented artist you are," he said, looking upon the scratchy work with every appearance of delight.

"Thank you." There was a stretch of silence, as she could think of nothing else to say. To apologize would be a disastrous admission of guilt.

"May I sit down?" he asked humbly at last.

She assented in some confusion, but made sure that there was plenty of distance between them on the stone bench. Lambrook sighed heavily. Madeline looked up in surprise and found that he was regarding her silently with a look of intense sadness in his dark eyes.

He must have seen the expression of surprise on her face, because he captured her hand and pressed it fervently. "Yes, Miss Delaney, I am miserable," he said in a low voice, then shrugged as he gave her an expressively rueful smile. "I have lost my one chance for happiness."

"Oh, dear, I had no idea that you were so fond of Lizzy!" she exclaimed, still thinking of his encounter with the housemaid and the lock.

A momentary look of confusion crossed his face, but he ignored her remark. "I have lost my one chance for happiness, because I have lost you." His hand began to caress hers, slowly.

Madeline drew it back, but did not chide him. His straight black brows were drawn together in such a tormented expression that she was concerned. "I do not understand what you mean." She watched him intently while he sat silently regarding the wisteria.

"I know who you are, Miss Delaney," he said

softly at last. At her sudden intake of breath, he turned to her. "You are the woman who has haunted my dreams. You are the woman from the ball. With that kiss in the garden you damned the rest of my life to fruitless longing." He moved a fraction of an inch closer to her. "My life became meaningless from that moment."

Madeline gave a sharp laugh. "Well, my life certainly changed from that moment too," she replied dryly.

Again he captured her hand. "Is this true?" he breathed out, "Dare I hope? Until now, my only wish was that I should be allowed to worship from afar the goddess of that moonlit night. . . ."

"Doing it rather brown, Lambrook," she said with a smile. "You had no idea who I was when I walked into the drawing room the other day."

"I did not," he admitted despondently. "I have no excuse. I know that by my error I have severed any chance I could ever have for happiness in this life." He ran a hand through his hair to produce a poetic disorder in the black curls. "My only plea is that I was in such a state of distraction. I would not have recognized my own brother. I have been blinded. Blinded by love."

Madeline exhaled with a noise that was very like a snort. "And why did you not propose to me when you had the chance?" she demanded with one raised brow.

He still possessed her hand and now pressed it to his chest. "Miss Delaney"—he sighed—"I am a coward. I was afraid. I have never been in love before, and the experience overwhelmed me. I fought it. Yes, I fought it valiantly. I felt as though I was possessed. I was unable to cloak myself in worldly cynicism; I could no longer hide beneath my shell of indifference. I had been vanquished. Slain by love. Brought to my knees by a slip of a girl . . ." Here he flung himself dramatically onto his knees. "I am no longer afraid. I am humbled by love." He looked up at her with an expression both pained and desperate. "Miss Delaney, please, marry me."

Madeline sat stunned for a moment. She felt an urge to laugh, but repressed it. Gently, she removed her hand from his impassioned grasp. "You honor me, milord," she said at last, "But I cannot—"

"Your father be damned, we shall run away!" Lambrook interjected desperately.

"I do not wish to run away."

"We shall get his consent somehow." His dark eyes flashed.

"It has nothing to do with that," she said impatiently. "I am flattered, but I do not wish to marry you."

"Ah!" he exclaimed tragically, "You cannot forgive me! I cannot forgive myself." He got up from his knees, dusted them carefully, and sat down again beside her. He was uncomfortably close, but as she was at the end of the bench, Madeline could not move away.

"I have frightened you with my passion," he announced, with a brooding sigh. "But Miss Delaney"—he regarded her intently with his hypnotically dark, veiled gaze—"I know that you, underneath your maidenly manners, are as passionate as I." He leaned forward, so close that she could smell the pomade he used on his hair.

Madeline leaned back as far as she dared. "Actually"—she laughed nervously—"actually, I think I am rather more impulsive than passionate."

"Then be impulsive." He breathed out the words, his arm snaking around her waist.

"No, I think I should go." She rose to leave, but he detained her.

"Madeline, I love you! Come with me to Gretna Green. I have a carriage waiting!"

"I thought your carriage was being repaired," she said, momentarily distracted.

"I have borrowed one of your uncle's. He will not mind. Come, fly with me." His arm tightened around her to an extent that was almost painful.

"I will not!" she exclaimed loudly. She punctuated this statement with a push so vigorous that she fell off the end of the bench and landed in an indignant froth of petticoats in a bed of lilies.

"I do not believe Miss Delaney is desirous of your attentions, Lambrook."

It was Forth. Madeline felt like crying with relief. She leapt up and shook her skirts out over her ankles. She would have liked to have flung herself into her rescuer's arms, but he looked positively fearsome.

"Oh"—Lord Lambrook had recovered enough

to laugh viciously—"it is the tutor come to play gentleman."

"You have overstayed your welcome. However, I am certain Miss Delaney will forgive your cretinous behavior if you beg her pardon and take leave of Elmhurst today."

"I am Lord Hesstrow's guest," Lambrook replied. "You are nothing but a hired servant. I shall have you dismissed for impertinence." Lord Lambrook rose to his feet, but his voice was still calm and sardonic.

"You have abused our hospitality too much, Lambrook. I hope you are prepared to find seconds. I am calling you out." Devin's expression was grimly serious.

"You?" Lambrook spat vitriolically "You are calling me out?" He laughed harshly. "You cannot. You are not a gentleman."

"I am of better breeding if not better blood than you, Lord Lambrook. I am certainly eligible to draw your cork. Shall we say tomorrow in the orchard? I will send my second to arrange the details." Grabbing the stunned Madeline none too gently by the elbow, he strode away in the direction of the house.

"Oh, Devin, I mean Mr. Forth . . . oh, dear. . . . You called him out . . . oh, dear . . ."

"Stop your babbling." He pushed her towards the side door of the house. "Go to your room. You have caused enough trouble today."

* * *

"Benny, what do you know about Lord Lambrook?" Madeline asked that evening as Mrs. Benjamin helped her get ready for bed. She had ventured downstairs to dinner only to find that the duke was indisposed and was having his dinner in his room. Mr. Forth was nowhere to be seen.

The older woman stopped putting curlpapers in Madeline's hair and regarded her in some surprise. "Nothing you should know, missy," she replied tartly.

"Oh. Well, if you mean about Lord Dancy's mistress, I already knew about that." She ignored Mrs. Benjamin's horrified ejaculation. "Does he gamble?"

"I don't know."

"I suspect he does."

Mrs. Benjamin frowned. "He is a bad egg in every respect. The less you know about him the better."

"Yes, but I was just wondering if you had heard any gossip about his financial situation."

"I never listen to gossip." Mrs. Benjamin replied, with a virtuous toss of her lace-topped head.

Madeline rose from the dressing table and drew her companion over to a settee. "I just thought perhaps you might have happened to have heard something." She settled herself companionably beside the woman.

"Humph!" Her duenna looked only slightly

mollified. "Well, I have heard it said that he is deeply in debt, indeed."

"Dun territory. . . ." Madeline mused. "I daresay that my marriage portion is large enough."

"What a vulgar comment! What can you possibly . . . ? You cannot. . . . Never say that. . . ."

Madeline cut short the woman's sputterings. "Of course not. The man is a fortune hunter. I have had undeniable evidence of that today."

Mrs. Benjamin waited for an explanation, but she was disappointed.

"I think I will get myself ready for bed, Benny. I need some time to think," she said, her expression rather distracted.

"Oh, but, pet, I am not done with your hair."

"I can finish it. Don't worry about me, I just need a moment to put my thoughts in order."

"You'll ring if you need anything?"

"Of course. Good night, Benny."

When she was alone, Madeline got up and began to roam the room. Lambrook had doubtless found out that her marriage portion was large. The sum must have been large enough to jar his memory at last. The events of the morning made her laugh now. He had been so desperate!

But then, there was the matter of the duel. Would it actually happen? Surely these things never really occurred. They were merely the blustering of male egos, finally settled amiably by one party apologizing and everyone going off for a pint of ale. She wanted very much to be present when Lambrook begged Mr. Forth's pardon.

But what if it did take place? Would they really meet with pistols at dawn? She envisioned Devin in a white shirt, splashed with blood and open at the neck, dying in her arms.

For a moment the notion seemed appealing, and then the reality of the situation swept over her with cold prickles. He might actually die, or at least be hurt, and even if he was not, he would be forced to leave the country. She would never see him again, and this was all happening on account of her silly indiscretion.

She dragged on a robe and ran barefoot down the hall and up the stairs to the small room where she knew he slept. It was the simplest thing. Once she explained that Lambrook was only hoping to dip his hands into her fortune, he would see how stupid the entire affair was and the whole thing would be forgotten.

"Mr. Forth!" She burst in without knocking. She was wild-eyed, her hair a jumble of curlpapers and pins. "You cannot do it! You shall be killed!" She was prepared to fling herself about his knees, but he stopped her with a gesture.

"No histrionics, please, Miss Delaney," he said tiredly, getting up from his desk.

"But, Devin! This is all my fault! I cannot allow you to do this."

"Please do not call me by my Christian name," he replied with unsettling calmness.

"But you do not understand! I know why Lambrook was courting me. He wants my dowry. He now remembers who I am and thinks that because of . . . well, because of that nonsense of my kissing him, I love him and he can have my fortune!" She smiled triumphantly, her hands held out to him.

He did not return her smile. "I am not in the least surprised to hear it," he replied.

"But, you see, now there will be no duel. He does not even have to apologize. Now that I know what all his playacting was about, I am not angry anymore. I only feel sorry for him. He did look very foolish, you know." She laughed. "I wish you could have heard him: 'I love you Madeline. I only want to worship at your feet." She imitated Lambrook's voice mockingly.

Mr. Forth turned back to his desk. "I am happy that you are appeased."

"So you will not fight?"

"On the contrary," he replied, not looking at her.

"Why?" she demanded angrily. "You won't! I won't let you!" She crossed the room to him, but he still did not look up.

There was a long silence. "It is a matter of honor now."

"Honor!" she said scornfully, "Who cares for that! He has no honor. I was not hurt, and the matter was of no significance. You are only letting your ego get in the way." She laughed. "Besides, I quite enjoyed having him throw himself at me."

Devin stood and regarded her with contempt.

"Well, I am glad that you enjoyed yourself, for it may well be the cause of his death."

"Pooh!" said Madeline scornfully, her former fear for his safety evaporated. "You are both acting like Frederick."

His scowl became practically murderous. "Your silliness has caused this to some extent," he snapped. "You are incorrigibly featherwitted. You encouraged the advances of a man you well know is capable of ruining you—with more than a few kisses." His voice rose. "Do you have any idea what could have occurred if I had not happened upon you? He would have kidnapped you! He had your uncle's closed coach waiting to drag you off to Gretna!" Forth advanced upon her and took her by the shoulders. "You are foolish and vain, and you have no idea of the kind of trouble you can cause!" He gave her a little shake and let her go. "If I were your father, I would lock you in a tower until you were seventy years old or showed some good sense. I have never met a more unmanageable, irresponsible, hoydenish chit!"

This was not the kind of meeting Madeline had anticipated. She stared at him, furious, humiliated and entirely speechless.

"I did it," she at last managed to whisper.

"Did what?" His voice was unpleasantly harsh.

"I locked him out of his room. While you are cataloging my faults, you should include that one. You told me not to plot any vengeance, but I did anyway. So you had better add vindictive and childish to your list. But perhaps you already said childish," she mused.

Mr. Forth's expression was absolutely murderous. There was nothing left to do but make a hasty retreat.

Eight

The day dawned, weak and sickly with a fog that threatened to turn into rain. Madeline had spent another sleepless night making and discarding plans to stop the meeting in the morning. She had even gone so far as to try and commandeer all of the firearms in the house, but quickly realized this, too, was fruitless, since presumably these men owned weapons of their own.

Why did they have to settle this matter like schoolboys? After all, she was the one with the quarrel with Lambrook, and now she no longer cared that he had accosted her. It seemed silly to make the incident anything more than trifling. But it was her honor they were fighting over. The entire notion was too pathetic and ridiculous since, if they had thought about it, neither of them cared enough for her to want to die for her. Good heavens, Lambrook probably wouldn't loan her a handkerchief. The thought of how Mr. Forth felt about her was even more depressing.

As soon as it was light enough to see, Madeline dressed quietly and without the aid of her maid.

She became more panicked with every passing moment, afraid that they might already have begun. Her walk toward the orchard turned into a run. She arrived breathless and in a state of disarray, relieved to find only Mr. Forth and the surgeon there. As there was no one lying on the ground and the surgeon appeared unoccupied, she decided that the duel had not yet begun. Devin scowled when he saw her.

"Why have you come?"

"I had to stop this stupidity! Please don't go through with it! I would never forgive myself." She was panting, but grabbed his sleeve with unexpected strength.

"I begin to fear that your theatrical speeches may be in vain, Miss Delaney—" he replied, detaching her from his arm. "Lord Lambrook appears to abhor violence as much as yourself."

"What do you mean?"

"He is nowhere to be found. Mr. Garring, my second, has gone in search of him."

Jeremy Garring himself arrived at this moment, a pistol case clasped casually under one arm, and confirmed the disappearance of the man in question. "He left in a hired coach from Wincanton late last night," he announced. Madeline recognized Garring from Lady Hesstrow's ball. He was the younger son of a large landholder in the district.

"He left?" she cried. "He is a coward!"

"Miss Delaney, you are unexpectedly bloodthirsty. Just moments ago you were begging me not to go through with it." Devin's expression was deceptively mild.

"Did you know he would not come?"

"I suspected."

"And you let me worry? You let me think you would be killed? How could you be so cruel?"

"The entire affair was really none of your concern," he replied.

"None of my concern? First, it was all my fault, and now it is none of my concern?" She felt like screaming with frustration, but Forth did not respond. He turned to Garring and the surgeon.

"Thank you both. Let us hope that this matter is happily forgotten." The surgeon looked quite crestfallen at the duel's cancellation, but he bowed elegantly and took leave of them. Devin silently offered his arm to Madeline, and the three who were left began to walk back to the house. "I would invite you in to breakfast, Garring, but I doubt there is any to be had at this hour. Besides, I would prefer to keep this matter quiet."

"Of course," Mr. Garring replied affably, as if the matter were no more than what he usually encountered before six o'clock in the morning. He bid them good-bye as they approached the house, and Devin and Madeline walked on in silence. She could not hold in her wrath for very long, however, and as soon as their companion was out of hearing, she voiced her annoyance in a torrent of abuse. Relief that the duel was not to take place somehow allowed all her fury to boil more freely. Mr. Forth, however, cut her off midrant with a curt bow.

"We shall speak of this when you are not so distraught."

"Of course I am distraught. You let me think you were going to die!"

"How little faith you have in my abilities," he commented coolly. He stopped and looked down at her. It was cold and still in the grove of trees by the house. The diffused early light made the place look different than she had ever seen it before.

She was suddenly aware that they were alone for the first time since that day in the dancing parlor. She felt her breath catch in her throat in a peculiar way and her heart pound like it had that afternoon, but she clenched her jaw and held her ground.

Devin stood silently beside her. "Miss Delaney," he began at last. His voice was low, and she could tell that he was no longer angry. That infuriating coolness was gone. "My behavior to you has been unconscionable. You, too, are a guest in this house, and I, as Lambrook said, am not a gentleman. I had no right to take you to task for any of your behavior. I have been overly familiar with you."

Madeline felt vastly disappointed. Somehow, even when they were quarreling, they had been equals and now he was trying to emphasize the differences between their stations. She finally raised her eyes to his. "I am very sorry for all of the trouble I caused you," she replied. "You saved me from a situation in the garden that had become extremely difficult. I was a little frightened."

He smiled, some of the warmth coming back to his gray eyes. "I cannot believe you have ever been afraid." He smiled wryly. "You just dislike not being able to be a meddling, conniving little creature." He said the words almost fondly. "I would offend your ears if you heard my opinion of the man. I am happy that you were unhurt, and that I could be of assistance. I thought when I first arrived in the garden that I was interrupting something of mutual interest. . . ."

Madeline could not help but laugh. Lambrook was far away and seemed bumbling and harmless. "He was like a leech! I could not keep him away. I have never met a man so persistent!"

"I confess, I did wait a moment out of sight to make sure that you really did need assistance. It was a very comic struggle. You should have simply told him to go to the devil." They were both laughing now, and Madeline reenacted the interlude with herself and Lambrook, playing both parts with such exaggerated mimicry that in retrospect the moment seemed much less frightening. Madeline could not forget that she had, at the time, been in a rather delicate situation and that Mr. Forth's intervention had been very timely.

"I was never so relieved to see you." She sighed, more serious now.

"I knew what a bounder he was. I knew that you had had trouble with him before and that he had taken advantage of your naïveté." Madeline bristled at this, but let him go on. "It gave me much pleasure to call him out."

"Oh, I really wish you had not. It was dreadful. I didn't think those kinds of things really happened."

"They should not. There are more civilized ways to settle things. However, I suspected that, in his heart, Lord Lambrook is callow and would only be frightened away with a serious threat of violence to his person."

"I wish I had known that! I was so worried! I truly thought you would be killed." Madeline had taken his arm, and they walked companionably through the trees. She was disappointed to note that they were very near the house now. She was not sure if it was he or she who stopped first. Devin suddenly appeared distressingly close to her.

"Would you have cared so much?" he asked softly.

"Yes." It was difficult to say even that one word when her body seemed intent on distracting her by trying to die. He took her by the shoulders, and she heard her own breath exhale sharply in something between a whimper and a moan. There was a moment of silence, and then something seemed to snap. Devin pulled her into his arms and kissed her fiercely.

Madeline was stunned for a moment and could not respond. Or at least she did not think she had responded, but she realized with surprise that she had wound her arms around his neck and was returning his passion. This was nothing like that awkward, sloppy experience with Lord Lambrook. Devin's kiss possessed her and gave her body a will and desire that were not her own. She pressed herself against him and felt his hand tighten on her back. His breath was coming as fast as her own as he deepened the kiss to a point where the darkness edged her consciousness.

And then it was over. Madeline was left clinging to his lapels, reeling and desperate for him. She closed her eyes and leaned her face closer to his, in the hope of encouraging him to kiss her again. She opened them only to discover that he was staring at her with a look of horror and repugnance. As humiliation flushed her features, she allowed him to disentangle himself from her arms.

"I am as much of a monster as Lambrook to take advantage of you like this." His face was drawn and his mouth a tight line. "I am worse. I am not even of your social standing. This will never, ever happen again Miss Delaney. You must believe me when I say I am very sorry I did that."

"But Mr. Forth," Madeline began, catching his sleeve, "you have entirely misunderstood."

"I think I do understand. I will stay away from you for the remainder of your stay here, and I will thank you if you will not seek me out."

"Please Devin! Don't—"

He pulled his arm from Madeline's grasp and strode quickly off toward the house. Without the support of his embrace, she leaned shakily against a tree. What was that supposed to mean? It was as if he had kissed her to punish her or to make a point, but if so, perhaps he had not kissed her thoroughly enough since she was still entirely confused.

She suddenly wished that Isabella was present. Perhaps men did this kind of thing all the time and it was some kind of cryptic social signal her teachers at the finishing academy had neglected to mention. Come to think of it, most of them were spinsters, so perhaps they had not even known about it. . . . She was tempted to race after him and insist that he explain in plain English what it was he'd meant, but his scowl had been so ferocious she did not think that approach was wise.

"Well, I think you should be happy, pet; Lord Lambrook seems to have taken himself off of his own accord." Mrs. Benjamin swept triumphantly into Madeline's room later that morning. She stopped in shock. "My dear girl, what is the matter?"

"Nothing, I am quite all right." Madeline ducked her head. "What were you saying about Lambrook?"

"Your face is flushed. You must have a fever. I knew it. I knew you were looking unwell yesterday."

"Really, Benny, I feel fine."

"Don't tell me what fine is. You with your eyes bright with fever." She felt Madeline's forehead.

"You don't feel too badly off, but I could tell in one look that you had a fever coming on."

"Don't be silly. It is only that I went for a . . . a . . . an invigorating walk this morning." It had certainly been that.

"Well, don't you let your aunt see you like that or she will be dosing you up or calling for that charlatan of a doctor of hers." Mrs. Benjamin pressed Madeline's cheek again and reluctantly conceded that she was not feverish.

"Lambrook is gone?" Madeline prompted, hoping to distract the woman from herself.

"Indeed. Gone this morning. Perhaps even last night. One of the grooms said he and that tiger of his rode their carriage horses to Wincanton. Who knows where they have gone. I hope to heaven it is far. There are not many places he can dare show his face these days, that wicked man."

Madeline agreed vaguely.

"The household is on its ear. Your aunt is near hysterics. Of course she has now convinced herself that Lambrook was a dear friend of the family, that he has simply abandoned us for no reason and has ruined the family's reputation throughout the countryside. The silly woman is half-mad as to what to do about her silly Venetian breakfast. Are you attending to anything I am saying, Madeline?"

"What? Oh, yes, certainly."

"Don't try to tell me you don't have a fever."

"Oh, but, Benny, I don't, I swear I don't. I was only thinking about how I would like to write Isabella to tell her of all our adventures. Do you

suppose that would be all right? You don't mind
if I just sit quietly and write a letter, do you, Benny
dear?"

Mrs. Benjamin eyed her with great suspicion.
"You won't be doing anything? I've known you
long enough to know that when you get all quiet,
you are planning something. You won't do anything to get into trouble?"

"Of course not, Benny." Madeline smiled an-
gelically, feeling as though she had gotten into
quite enough trouble for the day already.

She sat at her desk for nearly an hour, her pen
poised above a blank piece of paper. Desperate to
share these confusing experiences with someone,
she started the letter several times, but was always
frustratingly unable to put her feelings into words.
It did not help that all of her communication to
Isabella thus far had dwelled in expanded detail
upon the odious Mr. Forth's many faults. Reluctantly, she replaced the stopper on the ink and
gave up.

There was no way to talk about what had happened, and besides, it would be easier to explain
when there was something concrete to announce.
Vaguely, she chewed the tip of the pen, oblivious
to the black mark it made at the corner of her
mouth. However, it hardly looked as though Mr.
Forth was likely to propose or even to announce
his undying love for her. Wasn't that what men
were supposed to do after a kiss? This was most
provoking altogether. Either novelists like Mrs.
Radcliffe had it all wrong, or she herself had had

the shocking misfortune to be kissed by the only two unromantic, or misinformed men in the country. Perhaps it was only that they were not well read. Tossing the ruined pen into the fire, she sat in absorbed thought as it burned.

Surely Devin had meant something by that kiss. Surely he was not like Lambrook. He would not forget what had happened, and even if he did not love her, perhaps he could be relied upon to explain what had come over him so suddenly.

"Madeline! What are you doing?" Mrs. Benjamin's shrill voice cut into her thoughts. "What is that smell?"

"I am sorry, Benny." Madeline roused herself out of her reverie, "I forgot what I was doing and put a pen in the fire."

"Well, it is certainly too hot for a fire anyway. I should not have insisted on one today except that you looked so peaky the last few days. Oh, and the smell of burnt feathers!" She flapped her skirts ineffectually at the smoking hearth. "I thought for certain your aunt had fainted up here!" She laughed as though this were an exceedingly good joke. She stopped in alarm, seeing Madeline's lack of reaction. "Are you sure you are feeling quite the thing? You do not look like yourself."

"I am fine. Really. In fact, I think I will go downstairs and see my aunt." She examined herself intently in the mirror for a moment. "Would you help me change my dress?" she asked suddenly, rubbing vigorously at the ink mark at the corner of her mouth.

"Why?"

"Why shouldn't I? I don't care for this one." Madeline scowled.

"It is a bit early to change for dinner." Her duenna's brows rose in surprise. "Next you will be as bad as Lady Hesstrow, with a different gown for every hour of the day. A different gown for each of the chairs in her sitting room!" She laughed at herself again.

"Well, I am glad someone is in a good mood," Madeline replied peevishly.

Mr. Forth was extremely reticent. Not only did he refrain from proposing, embracing, or even darting loverlike glances at her, the odious man had disappeared altogether. As Lambrook's unexplained departure left the household in no small state of uproar, no one commented on the absence of the tutor. Madeline supposed that someone knew where he was, but she was not about to ask after him. It was obvious that he did not want to be found. It was beyond humiliating to have been kissed and rejected by two men in the space of less than two months.

But the next day passed and there was no word of him. The dancing lessons ceased with no prior notice, and he did not appear at the dinner table. Having worn all of her best dresses for no reason, Madeline at last acquiesced to defeat and mounted the stairs to the schoolroom. It was empty, but out of the window, she spied Frederick, up in a tree. She tried to call to him, but he did not hear, so she went outside to find him.

"What are you doing?" she asked when she found the elm that contained him.

"Making a rabbit trap," he replied, still absorbed in tying the rope he held around the branch of the tree.

"Rabbits don't live in trees."

Frederick cast down a look of scorn. "Of course not. This is a trap I invented. See, the rabbit"—here he paused and scampered down the tree—"the rabbit is hopping along"—he demonstrated this—"and it sees this carrot!" He produced the object from his pocket. "And the carrot is lying here, holding down the rope and the branch." He now flexed the branch down by pulling the rope and attempted to weight it down with the carrot.

The demonstration was unsuccessful and succeeded only in flinging the carrot into the bushes and showering Frederick with leaves. "Well, see, the rabbit was supposed to step into a loop made with the rope, to eat the carrot, and then once he ate it, he would get whipped up by the rope because the carrot would be lighter. Because he ate it, you see. I need a bunch of carrots," he announced, retrieving the old one from the bushes.

"It's a terribly clever idea," Madeline said generously. She watched for a moment in silence as he attempted to reset the trap. "Shouldn't you be having lessons?" she asked at last.

"No," he replied cheerfully. She waited, but he did not offer any information as to the whereabouts of his tutor.

"Where is Mr. Forth?" she inquired with what she hoped was nonchalance after her cousin had completed another unsuccessful springing of the rabbit trap. It was obvious that any attempts to lead to the topic with subtlety would be lost on him.

"I dunno," he replied calmly. Then he stopped and thought a moment. "He left."

"Left?"

"He went home."

"Home?" Madeline echoed in surprise "Why?"

"I dunno," Freddie replied recalcitrantly. "I think someone died and he went home for the funeral." This was the most information she could get out of him, so she left him pensively regarding the carrot in a shower of leaves. Mrs. Benjamin met her at the door.

"I have a letter for you, my dear!" she sang out. "It is from your father." Madeline took it and read it with a mixture of emotion. The prime minister, Spencer Perceval, had been shot in the lobby of the House of Commons, and the city was in turmoil. It was believed that this was a plan of the radicals to overthrow the current government. The Luddite riots, which had begun in Nottinghamshire the previous fall had spread across the country with angry mobs of laborers breaking the machines that stole their trades from them and assaulting landowners. Although he was sure that her aunt and uncle were taking the best care of her, at this time of unrest he wished for her to come back to London.

Madeline had never known Mr. Perceval, but she was sorry to hear of his death. It did, however, leave her in a difficult position. She had been at Elmhurst for six weeks and the season was just now at its peak. She longed to see Isabella again and to have more for company than Mrs. Benjamin, her aunt and uncle, and Frederick. Mr. Forth was the problem. How could she go when he himself had not yet returned. She could not leave when she suspected that she might be in love with him! But perhaps, if he did not care for her, it would be less humiliating if she were gone. They had left on such a strange footing. . . . If only he had explained that kiss!

Nine

"Excuse me, my lord," the butler said for the fourth time.

As this repetition was rather more loud and pointed, Devin turned around. "I am sorry, Bryant, I did not realize that you were speaking to me." He smiled sheepishly.

Bryant did not respond. Everything in his bearing indicated that he did not approve of lords who could not seem to remember their station and especially those who would commit the dual appalling acts of both apologizing and smiling at the servants. "Your estate manager, Mr. Redmond, is here to see you."

Mr. Redmond appeared behind Bryant's shoulder. He was a full head taller than the butler and had kinky red hair that made him appear even taller. He grinned. "Still having trouble remembering who you are?" he inquired jovially.

"I can't seem to get used it," the new Earl of Somerton replied, with a gesture that helplessly encompassed the entire room. Bryant bowed himself out, frowning so much that his whole head became a mass of lumps and furrows. Devin gestured to a chair. "How are things?"

"Very well. Very well, indeed." Redmond seated himself carefully, obviously hoping not to dirty the cushions of the chair. "Those extra men you hired are working out fine. They were just what we needed for the reroofing. I expect there won't be any troubles on that account when it comes time for harvest. Your tenants are relieved, I can tell you that. For the last fifteen years, everything they grew was rotted with the wet from leaky storehouse roofs inside of three months."

"Well, I am happy to hear that things are being accomplished. I will ride out tomorrow and see some of your work myself. I have perfect confidence in your abilities, but—"

"I understand entirely, your lordship. The tenants will be pleased you are taking such a personal interest in their welfare." Redmond gave a gruff laugh, but his eyes were sincere.

"I would not have known what needed to be done if it were not for your guidance. I am afraid that I am a sad hand at estate management."

Redmond's smile disappeared in an expression of bitterness. "You'll be better than the one before you, if you'll beg my pardon. I have been managing here since I was five and twenty, and I can't tell you how much it has broken my heart to see this place go to pieces. Money spent on nothing but horseflesh. Now I can appreciate a good goer myself, but when the buying of them starts to take the food out of the mouths. . . ."

He shook his head. "Well, it was horseflesh that did him in in the end anyway." He said grimly, referring to the death of Devin's cousin in a hunting accident.

"In any case, I am glad things are going well." Devin turned from the subject in a pleasant tone. "I was hoping, Redmond, you could recommend to me someone who might be suitable for the post of housekeeper."

The estate manager gave him his characteristic snaggletoothed grin. "I am sure I could find someone for you. But my wife won't be too happy about it."

"Why is that? Was she hoping for the position?"

"She is hoping that you will take a wife. She says there is no use in smartening up the estate and tenant's houses when your own house is falling in around your ears. It wants the touch of a lady." He laughed. "Now I am sure you had plenty of young things running after you before you came here, but now, as Mrs. Redmond has been telling me, as you are the new Earl of Somerton, you are prime material on the marriage mart!" He laughed for a long time at this, but Devin joined in only halfheartedly.

Madeline was again ensconced in front of the mirror in her London home, having her hair dressed by Mrs. Benjamin. Her father had welcomed her back with open arms and had insisted that she stay up hours after she was stifling yawns so that he could hear the news of her uncle's estate and analyze in an excruciating monologue the changes the new government would bring.

In her own small corner of the world, less important, but equally remarkable events had occurred. Mr. Adleson and Lord Turner were both engaged. Lord Houndsheath was rumored to have taken up with a widow, and of course the interesting Mr. Johnson had run off with that scandalous woman. Maria Lucciono was no longer in vogue as the soprano songbird and masked balls were all the rage.

Her father had insinuated that the stress of her first season had made her unwell, but that seemed patently false, since she had last been seen dancing out the French doors with the dashing Lord Lambrook. However. . . . She peered at her face in the glass. She was thinner and paler than she had been when she'd left, and there was a listlessness in her formerly buoyant nature. Perhaps people would indeed be fooled as to the cause of her departure. Mrs. Benjamin herself was currently grumbling under her breath about how young ladies who were ill shouldn't be made to stay out till all hours at a ball.

"Actually, I am feeling a little peaked. Perhaps I should stay home and rest," she said faintly, attempting to look even more tired than she felt, though she knew she was succumbing to cowardice. "I am sure I will feel well enough to attend Lady Pembroke's masked ball at the end of the week." Her voice was so theatrically faint that Mrs.

Benjamin's expression changed instantly from complete sympathy to suspicion.

"You needn't stay too long," she said, casting a sharp eye on Madeline's response.

Madeline gave in. "I know I am being a mealy-mouthed nitwit. It . . . it has just been so long since I was out in public. And I don't want to be cut or something terrible like that on account of the Incident." She widened her eyes pleadingly at Mrs. Benjamin. The duenna looked as though she might waver, but Madeline forced herself not to take advantage of her companion's sympathy. She sat up straighter. "Never mind, Benny. I will go. I should get it over with." And with that she stood up and marched out of the room, her slim shoulders so straight and stiff, she appeared to be going out to meet the lions.

The "small affair" included almost three hundred people, and so after passing smilingly through the receiving line, Madeline intended to retire quietly to an obscure corner. She felt slightly stunned and dizzy in the light of two dozen blazing chandeliers. They reflected wildly off the polished floor rapidly filling with dancers, off the long gilded mirrors of the side walls, and off the silks and jewels of so many glittering people. It was hard to believe that things were always like this, and know that not six weeks ago she had been not only blasé about it, but a part of it.

She had not made it halfway across the room

before she was assailed by Sir George and several of his friends. They reminded her of a litter of puppies as they bounded around her, exclaiming how happy they were that she had returned and that it had been deadly dull without her. Sir George was wearing his usual dazzled expression. He managed to get out several half sentences of relatively no sense before Mrs. Benjamin, wearing her best duenna frown, latched herself to Madeline's arm and continued to forge on ahead to a settee in an alcove.

Madeline relaxed slightly, grateful that she had not been cut, at least by the male portion of the guests. Overall, she realized after some time, people treated her as though nothing had happened. The few that actually realized she had been absent commented solicitously about her health, but did not seem overcurious. She felt her anxiety melt away and began to enjoy herself as she was escorted off to dance with gratifying immediacy.

It was some time later, after she had danced several country dances, that Isabella arrived. Her parents, nothing like the serious, brown-eyed girl, were chronically extravagant and always late. Isabella looked slightly harried, but hurried to her friend. After they embraced, they sat down together on the settee.

"Oh, Madeline, I am so sorry I did not write you more often. I know I should have, especially when you were so far away all alone." Isabella looked contrite and uncomfortable. "I know I should have called on you yesterday or today, even though they were not your at-home days, but . . . I thought that you might be tired from your journey." She flushed to the roots of her hair. "I am lying. I was ashamed to come see you, because . . . because it had been so long since I had written you."

"Bella, it was my fault. I should have written more, too," Madeline replied lightly, surprised that her friend seemed so uncomfortable. Why, the girl was practically shredding her handkerchief. "What has happened since I left?"

"Well, as I told you in my few letters, no one said much about your leaving. The few people who did approach me seemed fairly satisfied when I said you were ill. When Frances Chandler insinuated that you had left because of something that had happened between you and Lord Lambrook, I tried to look shocked and said that I was sure I would have known about that if it had been true."

Madeline laughed. "What an actress you have turned out to be! Thank you." She squeezed her friend's hand.

"But Maddie, you do look as though you have been ill. What has happened to you? The last time we wrote things were going well. . . ."

"I will tell you all about my adventures tomorrow. They are too long to be explained tonight. Tell me what have you been doing." She saw Isabella's eyes flicker for an instant toward Sir George and wondered if that romance had blossomed in her absence. However, she could see that Isabella's expression was unhappy, though her friend ducked her head to hide it. They talked a few minutes more about their various mutual acquaintances, and then George came up to blushingly ask Madeline to dance. He did not look at Isabella, who appeared to be transfixed by something across the room.

"I am very happy that you are back," he began, grinning like an idiot. "You look absolutely more beautiful than a gem."

"Thank you." She smiled up at him, able to keep a straight face only because laughing seemed to take too much effort. When the movements of the dance brought them together again, George leapt straight to the point.

"May I call upon you?"

"What?" She looked at him with a vague expression.

"May I call upon you?" he repeated, his pale red brows drawn together in concern over her obvious preoccupation.

"Of course, Sir George. I would enjoy that very much. However. . . ." Here she was forced to wait again for the complicated steps to reunite them. When they did, she had lost courage. She desperately decided to postpone the interview. "I would like to speak to you for a moment after this dance is over."

"Oh, yes, Miss Delaney," he breathed out, obviously in raptures.

When the dance did end, Madeline had galvanized her resolution. She took his arm and led him toward a cluster of potted palms that was somewhat private, while still being in the view of Mrs. Benjamin. "Sir George. I know that I may be being presumptuous and vain, but I would like to be frank with you."

This was easier than she had thought it would be, not because she did not care about George's feelings, but because, since leaving Elmhurst, she felt it hard to feel anything but a cotton-woolly numbness, much like the time when she had had laudanum for a tooth extraction. And like the dental experience, she knew that once the numbness went away, it was going to hurt. "I care very much for you as a dear friend, but my feelings go no further than that. I am sorry if I have led you on in the past." She stopped, waiting for his reaction. He looked perplexed, but not upset.

"I am grateful to you for your honesty, Miss Delaney." He smiled. "You know that I have admired you for a long time and that I would have continued to pursue you if I thought I could win you. However, I am happy to continue our relationship as friends." He bowed low over her hand. Madeline peered carefully into his face to assess the sincerity of this gallant speech, but his expression was calm. She was baffled, but relieved. Poor Sir George had never really understood the rules of the game, and she had always felt a bit guilty about keeping him enthralled, especially when she'd had an inkling that Isabella was sweet on him.

Feeling light and slightly self-satisfied, she rejoined the group, expecting Isabella and Sir

George to obligingly pair off to everyone's satisfaction. However, he took leave of them on his own and did not join their party for the rest of the evening. Madeline's own smugness was exploded when Isabella became stiff and cool, although she remained by her side and attempted to be good company.

After several agonizing hours, Madeline conveyed a message that she wished to leave via pleading eyes and lifted brows to Mrs. Benjamin. Her legs were aching from the dancing, as she was used to practicing only an hour and a half a day with Mr. Forth and Frederick. The memory of this annoyed her, and she wanted nothing more than to go home, fling herself across her bed, and feel very sorry for herself. However, she found that once the carriage had brought them home, she was far too exhausted to do anything more than sleep.

Over the next days she received several callers, a few of whom were important enough that their presence assured her welcome back into society. In some ways, she was delighted to be back in the whirl of the season, as she had missed her father and there was rarely a moment in which she had nothing to do. However, every party was so much the same as the next, and there was only a finite amount of excitement one could muster over the new cut of a pelisse or the shade of green that was all the rage. But this sameness blended the weeks of the season before the time at Elmhurst and during the time after into a continuum, so that often it seemed perhaps she had never been there at all.

It would have been easy to be caught up in her own heartbreak, had it not been for Isabella. She had been so strange lately. There were times when their relationship seemed as close as it had been before, yet at other times her friend seemed distant and secretive. Finally, Madeline confronted her.

"Isabella, is something worrying you?" she asked as they were on their way through the park on their weekly outing to the lending library.

"Worrying me? Why no!" replied Isabella, looking guilty and more worried than ever.

"Won't you please tell me? You seem so terribly unhappy." They had stopped, and Isabella allowed herself to be led to a park bench on which she sat down heavily and with an anguished sigh.

"It's Sir George," she said at last, her face slowly growing an unfortunately unflattering and shiny red that clashed with her shell pink muslin walking dress. "He . . . I . . . I love him." She gave a loud, half-hysterical laugh and began to cry. Madeline did not know what to say. This certainly was not a revelation to her.

"Is that all?" She tried not to sound impatient.

"No, it is not all." Isabella sat up straight and looked positively fierce. "Madeline, I realized that I loved him after you left, and I flirted with him shamelessly while you were gone."

Madeline's brows flew up. It was hard to imagine Isabella being coy. "Good for you!" she exclaimed with some admiration. Isabella stared at her in horror.

"But he was your beau! I tried to steal him."

"He was never my beau!" Madeline protested, "I never cared for him. I'm delighted you spent time with him while I was . . . away. I think you are both just perfect for each other." Isabella really must be a ninny to think she had ever harbored a tendre for Sir George.

"How could you not care for him?" Her friend seemed nearly insulted instead of relieved. "He is the dearest—" She broke off on another painful blush. "He is the dearest man that ever lived!" She appeared to be trying on and discarding moods faster than Madeline could ever keep up. Bewildered, Madeline tried another tactic.

"Has he proposed to you?"

"No." Isabella instantly dove into humiliated despondency. "Oh, Maddie, Everything was going so well until you returned! He took one look at you at the Grovesend ball and was dazzled all over again. I was never so jealous in all my life!" She looked prepared to cry again, so Madeline quickly flung her arms around her friend to dam the flood.

"No, Bella! It is you he loves! I am sure of it! Sir George thinks of me only as a friend." She almost told her of the conversation with Sir George, but decided that it might be hurtful. Isabella would always feel as though she were his second choice. "I have not seen him in nearly a week except at balls and routs, and he has only danced with me twice," she continued. "Surely he has called on you?"

"Yes." Isabella nodded and sniffed

"Then surely he means to propose."

Isabella paused and thought a moment. "I think so," she admitted candidly.

Madeline managed with difficulty to control her impatience, as Isabella, with uncharacteristic gregariousness, analyzed everything Sir George had ever said to her. She was stunned that two people with any wits about them could not simply realize their couplish perfection, get married, and be done with it. This made her wonder if she herself would ever meet someone whose temperament complemented her own like two puzzle pieces. Of course, this thought led to recalling Mr. Forth, which made her feel like shouting at strangers in the park that the world was nastily unfair.

Ten

"Mr. Forth!" It was Frederick, not the butler who opened the door to him at Elmhurst. The boy appeared to be about to fling himself into his former tutor's arms, but decided at the last moment that he was far too mature for any display of this kind. He satisfied his need to welcome Devin by leaping about and yelping with an enthusiasm very much like that of a very large and affectionate dog. The housekeeper fluttered in, rolling her eyes and flapping her hands.

"Mr. Forth! What are you doing here? I thought you were . . . Oh, but you are Lord Somerton now!"

"Forgive me for dropping in on you so unexpectedly, Mrs. Stack. I was hoping I would still be welcome, despite my change in status." He smiled sheepishly.

"As if you would not always be welcome here! Even the young master is happy to see you." She laughed at the boy's exuberant cavortings. "I should have got the door myself, but things have been in such an uproar since you left. Master

Frederick saw you from the upstairs window and was quick as a wink." She squeezed Frederick around the shoulders affectionately. "I will tell Lord Hesstrow that you are here." Mrs. Stack ushered him into the blue sitting room and allowed Frederick to stay with him only at that young man's very vocal insistence.

"So, Lord Somerton, you have returned," Lord Hesstrow boomed as he entered the room. "I must get used to your new title!" He laughed as though this were a good joke. "I am delighted. Things have not been the same since we seem to have lost half our household." He noted Devin's bemused expression and explained. "My niece Madeline was called home immediately after you left. We are suddenly reduced to just Lady Hesstrow and Frederick and myself. Let's go into my study and have some cognac. I never could abide this silly, frilly room."

"Thank you, sir. Actually . . . I was just hoping to find out how you were getting on. I most likely cannot stay long," Devin protested as he followed his former employer. Frederick accompanied them, begging that he might have spirits too.

"Nonsense, you don't drive half a day just to find out how people are getting on." Lord Hesstrow poured an extremely generous tumbler of water and added a drop of cognac for color. This he handed to Frederick, who was now pleading that he might be allowed to smoke. Lord Hesstrow cocked a formidable brow at him and poured more substantial drinks for himself and Somerton. "My boy here has been lost without you."

"I am glad not to have those stupid dancing lessons," Frederick volunteered brightly. He took a large gulp of his drink and put the glass down in disgust.

"Did Miss Delaney go back to London to her father?" Lord Somerton asked, examining the contents of his glass intently.

"Yes, she did. And it is a good thing too. Enid was planning another party of some kind or another with that chit as an excuse. I don't know why her father wanted her back. Perhaps she told him of all the balls and routs and such fluff that Enid was cooking up. She looked more peaked when she left than when she came here. Now, I don't mind having a hunting party here in the fall, but these touted-up dancing parties where we must spend a fortune on food and dresses and all that folderol are just nonsense.

"And, of course, we were happy that Lord Lambrook took himself off. Demmed awkward of him to be here, what with him not being received in London and with that business with the chambermaid. Enid kicked up about it. Said he ruined her parties and all that kind of thing, but overall we were glad he left. I suppose it could have been worse. We haven't heard hide nor hair of him since. Went to the continent most likely. I heard he was rather badly dipped. Then there was that business with Dancy's mistress which I don't like to mention in front of Enid. Yes, indeed, a good thing he went. Demmed bad judge of horseflesh that man. Did you see those bays of his? Touched in the wind they were."

Before Devin was called upon to expound on this theme, begun by an unusually gregarious Lord Hesstrow, his wife made her appearance.

"My dear Lord Somerton! How wonderful that you have come to see us. And how wonderful that you feel you do not have to stand on ceremony and let us know beforehand. Do say that you will stay. We can host a lovely cotillion for you. Ah, yes, to celebrate your new status. How marvelous that our estates have always been so close together. We will see each other quite all the time."

"Actually, I must be on my way."

"But, Lord Somerton, you can't possibly be leaving. We were under the impression that this was a real visit. You must surely stay the week out," Enid insisted, laying her hand on his arm in the most friendly of manners.

"I am sorry that you misunderstood. I am on my way to London, and I only stopped to see how everyone was getting on. I really must be on my way today." Devin decided it was getting away from Lady Hesstrow's obvious toad-eating that inspired him to head unexpectedly toward the capital.

"Oh, but you cannot go today. If you must go, wait until tomorrow. You will not get far tonight, and you will have to stay in some unpleasant inn. We are always happy to have your company."

"I am afraid that my business compels me to

leave immediately," he lied, "but I could not resist coming to thank you again for your generosity to me." He said this to Lord Hesstrow with all sincerity. "By allowing me to stay here, you saved my sisters from having to take positions of their own." He shook Edmund's hand warmly.

"I must meet them gels sometime," Lord Hesstrow replied gruffly. "I know you sent home to them everything I paid you. I like to know where my money goes!" He laughed, obviously uncomfortable with Devin's thanks. Lady Hesstrow shot her husband a killing look.

Although Frederick was devastated at his departure, Devin salved his guilt by promising the boy that once he was settled, he would have him up for a visit. "Then I can show you all of the places we talked about when we learned history."

"The Tower? Can we go to the tower?" the boy demanded, nearly knocking over furniture in his excitement.

"Of course," Devin agreed. "And we will see the show at Astley's as well if you would like." This sent the boy into whoops, and Devin slipped out to pay a visit to the kitchen staff before Frederick could wreak major structural damage on the room.

"Are you certain you want to head to London tonight, my lord?" Lord Somerton's valet asked doubtfully.

"Yes, we might as well make a start of it," he replied.

"I wish your lordship had told me that we were

going to London. I was certain that your lordship had told me to pack only to go to Elmhurst. I have not included any clothing suitable for London."

"That is because, Perkins, I do not own anything suitable for London. I shall have some things made up once we are there. Allow me to be spontaneous this once."

Perkins's expression was dour. "And you wish to start out for London right now, my lord?" he asked again, obviously hoping for a different answer.

"I do. I find myself very anxious to settle my cousin's London affairs and to see if the town house is at all acceptable." He frowned in his best lordly style.

Perkins nodded reluctantly and climbed up to sit with the driver, since he suffered from motion sickness when within a carriage. Devin was glad to have the time to himself. He felt a need to pull his thoughts together.

Isabella darted into the room, closed the door behind her. "Madeline, it has happened!" she exclaimed breathlessly.

"What has happened?" Madeline leapt up from her seat in the windowsill where she had been watching the carriages pass.

"I"—Isabella lowered her voice conspiratorially—"have been kissed." She hugged herself and spun around the room.

"Really? How did it happen?" Madeline laughed. "How highly improper!"

"I know!" her friend squealed. "And it was nothing like you said it was."

"What do you mean?" She gave a guilty start.

"With Lambrook. The whistling nose and all that. It was nothing like your experience." Isabella heaved a gusty sigh. "It was perfect."

Madeline's throat tightened at the memory of the willow grove.

"It was after you went home with the headache from the rout at the Cowpers'. No one was watching, and he drew me into an alcove and . . . it just happened!"

"Was he angry with you?"

"What? Of course not. Why would he kiss me if he was angry with me?"

"I don't know." Madeline shrugged. "I just wondered."

"It was so very nice. I thought my knees would melt."

"And afterward?"

"He, well, he apologized. He said that he was wrong to have taken advantage of me."

Madeline perked up. "Did he?"

"But then he kissed me again!"

"Oh." Her brows drew together.

"Do you think that means he loves me?" Isabella looked anxious.

"I'm sure I don't know." Madeline's gaze went back to the window, and she scowled faintly.

"Oh, dear! Oh, heavens! Don't tell me—"

Madeline's reverie dissolved. "That I myself love Sir George? Don't be a widgeon. We already had this discussion! Of course Sir George loves you. How could anyone help it?"

"Well, he did say that he had something important to ask me. . . ." She drew out her handkerchief and began twisting it. "And he did ask when my father would be back from Yorkshire. That must mean that he intends to ask Papa for permission. . . ." Her voice trailed off hopefully.

"Of course it does," Madeline reassured her stoutly.

"I *think* he would have asked me right then, but he wants to ask Papa first. He is so funny about etiquette in that way. It rather reminded me of your dancing master."

"What?" Madeline's gaze jerked from the window again.

"The dancing master at Elmhurst who was so very prim and proper. The one who was always prosing on about propriety and etiquette. You wrote me about him remember?"

"I suppose I did," she replied vaguely.

"He sounded so very romantic. Even if he was stuffy. The poor disowned grandson of some Earl or another. . . ." Isabella sighed. "You said he was mysterious and tortured, remember? Was he really? How very poetic. Do you think he wrote poetry? You described him so vividly. I can't conceive why you did not fall in love with him yourself. . . ."

Madeline rose suddenly and crossed the room

to ring the bellpull. "I shall have some tea up to celebrate. You will be a married woman by next year, I'll wager."

Isabella gave a joyful squeak. "Do you think so?"

"Undoubtedly. When does your father return?"

"Three more days." She sighed. "It seems like forever. I am not at all sure how I will face Sir George today. I am glad you said that you would join the boating party. I think I would die with embarrassment if I had to face him alone after last night." She was lost for a moment in pleasurable contemplation. "And then there is the masked ball tonight."

"I am not sure I will go tonight," Madeline announced suddenly as she dropped tiredly onto a chair.

"Not go?" Isabella looked up in surprise. "Oh, but, Maddie, you must. You have not yet been to a masked ball, and it is so much fun. It is just the kind of thing you most enjoy."

"You mean being able to act as outlandish as I like without fear of recognition?" her friend asked with a wry smile. "Perhaps I would enjoy it. I just don't feel much like going."

"Why not?" Isabella peered at her suspiciously. "Are you feeling quite the thing? You have been so strange lately."

"I am just out of sorts," Madeline replied peevishly, "I am trying to stay out of trouble. I am bored. I am suffering from ennui." She laughed at herself and pressed the back of her hand to her forehead in a dramatic gesture. "I am going into a decline."

"I should have thought you would have been more bored in Somerset. Aren't you happy to be back? Oh, look! There is Lord Stedtson out driving his new bays. I suppose they are very fine, as everyone is talking about them."

"I imagine he paid a good deal too much for them. He would pay anything for a chance to show off."

"He is quite dreadful, isn't he? But I see that Frances is out with Lord Erickson. What a marvelous new bonnet she is wearing. I declare, it is positively covered with fruit. I know it sounds ghastly, but it really does look well."

"You are right, it is very fine." Madeline joined her at the window and scrutinized the bonnet.

"Here is Sir George at last. Do go get your bonnet, Maddie. And thank you again for being so kind about George. You must be bored to flinders with hearing about it. It makes me so happy that there is no awkwardness between all of us."

"Of course there is not."

Isabella flew to the mirror above the mantel and smoothed her hair. She saw in the reflection over her shoulder that Madeline had leaned her forehead onto the windowpane and was gazing out the window with an expression of such pensive sadness that she was alarmed. "Do come to the ball tonight. I cannot stand the thought of you moping about alone. It will be such fun," she cajoled, "and you never know who you might meet. Some handsome, masked stranger, perhaps?"

Madeline raised a skeptical eyebrow, but laughed. "I will go. I could not miss the chance to meet my one true love."

She felt that her heart had stopped beating. It was him. She was thankful that the hood of her domino obscured her face so she could stare without causing notice. The man over near the door to the card room was too like Mr. Forth to be anyone else but him. At first she'd thought it a result of her fevered imagination. But no, even with his eyes hidden by the mask, it was unmistakably Devin.

But he looked so different that she wondered for a moment if perhaps he had a brother or twin. His dark hair seemed darker, and he somehow seemed taller and more broad in the shoulders in his black domino. He was so out of context among this masked crowd of revelers; with his expensive clothes and graceful bearing, he did not seem to be the familiar Devin at all. Why would he possibly be in London? Why was he at Lady Pembroke's ball? Why did he not come speak with her?

Her body reacted faster than her still-reeling mind; her heart dropped to her stomach and began to pound furiously. She intended to draw back a moment and compose her thoughts, but feeling her gaze, he looked up and saw her. Their eyes locked, and for a breathless moment he was expressionless. She thought she saw a momentary flicker of surprise cross his face, but he quickly recovered and advanced upon her. His expression was unreadable as he bowed over her trembling hand.

"Would you care to dance, Miss Delaney?" His voice seemed so natural and calm! Madeline nodded, not trusting her own voice, and allowed him to lead her to the floor where a set was forming. She felt dazed, as though she had just stepped out into the sun on a bright day. She vaguely registered that the partner on her dance card for this dance was regarding them with some annoyance. Mrs. Benjamin, glancing up from her gossip, looked as though her eyebrows would disappear into her hairline.

"You recognized me," she said after a moment, indicating her scarlet domino with disappointment.

"Of course."

"Why are you here?" she asked, realizing after the words had left her mouth that they sounded rude.

His expression stiffened, but he did not reply at once. The dance commenced, and it was quite some time before the figures brought them back together. "I am here for a very short time to see the sights in London." He stated coolly.

"But how did you get into this party?" she asked incredulously. "It is quite exclusive."

If it were possible, her partner's manner became

even more aloof and cold. To her surprise, he looked down his nose at her with the most disdainful and superior of expressions. "I think I will choose to leave that remark unaddressed," he remarked at last and did not again speak to her for the rest of the set. He led her back toward Mrs. Benjamin and did not appear to be likely to break his silence, so she held him back slightly.

"I did not mean to sound as though I were not glad that you are here. I was simply surprised."

"Indeed. I am quite out of my element here." His word were clipped to an edge.

Forcing down a feeling of impatience, Madeline tried again. "You misunderstand me, Mr. Forth. I was simply surprised that the Hesstrows should allow you . . . I mean, I am surprised to see you in London."

"I am like Cinderella. Tomorrow I will be back at Elmhurst, blacking the Hesstrows' boots." His cynical expression was very unpleasing.

"I don't know why you are being so vicious to me. I am the one who has a right to be piqued. You disappeared entirely, without even telling me that you were leaving or where you were going!" It was only with the greatest restraint that Madeline refrained from stomping her foot.

"I apologize." Lord Somerton bowed over her hand with exaggerated grace. "Did you need your boots blacked while I was gone?"

"You have become an insufferable, affected, horrid creature since I saw you last!" she hissed, enraged.

Somerton regarded her with a look of pure loathing. "And you, dear Miss Delaney, have not changed one whit."

Eleven

The room suddenly seemed unbearably hot, and Madeline could feel the pressure of her frustration building into a headache in her temples. Sweetly begging leave for a moment in the lady's retiring room, she again abandoned poor Mr. Beaudet, then paced the hallways upstairs wondering what had just happened to her.

Devin was here in London, but he was not the man she had known at Elmhurst. This man was fierce, cold, and defensive. If he had not come here because he cared for her, why had he made an appearance in town and sought her out at a ball? At this point she was pacing at a furious and unladylike rate. Worse, she was nibbling the nail of her first finger. She forced herself to put her gloves back on and sit down in a chair in the abandoned upstairs parlor.

For some time she entertained the hope that Devin would come to find her and that everything would be sorted out. He did not appear. By now, her worrying had changed tack, and she had concluded that to him she was merely a silly chit in a scrape, willing to have a little flirtation while she was in the country. Surely he had seen the adoration on her face when she had first seen him tonight, and the idea that she had thrown her cap over the windmill for him was annoying.

She was deeply ashamed and humiliated, but at this point there was nothing left to do but return to the ballroom, since she had been missing for far too long. Someone would soon come looking for her to find out what was wrong. Squaring her shoulders and scowling so fiercely that it was comical, she descended again into the ballroom.

Devin was not there. She managed to finish out the evening, and if anyone noticed that she laughed too loudly or that her eyes sparkled strangely or that her mouth was fixed in a smile that never changed, they did not comment. Finally, guests began to leave and Madeline allowed herself to ask a footman for her and Mrs. Benjamin's cloaks.

Her companion said nothing as they waited for the carriage to be brought around, but once they were within its private confines, she began. "I wonder that Lord Somerton did not spend more time speaking with you. He might at least have gotten you a glass of punch."

"Lord Somerton?" Madeline asked blankly.

"Lord Somerton, Mr. Forth. Don't tell me you did not recognize him in his domino!"

"Lord Somerton?" Madeline repeated with

growing apprehension. She felt uncomfortably as though someone had been playing a cruel joke on her.

"Mr. Forth, Frederick's tutor from Elmhurst—"

"I know who he is," Madeline snapped.

"—has recently inherited a title," Mrs. Benjamin continued placidly. "William Forth, whom you wouldn't have met, my dear, as he was rarely in Town and spent an inordinate amount of time at his hunting box or his grouse moor in Scotland, died last May in a hunting accident. Tragic really. Forth is the heir. Most people didn't know it because the former Lord Somerton, Forth's grandfather, practically disowned his younger son for running off and marrying some woman of whom he did not approve. But there it is. Lady Hesstrow must be in fits." Mrs. Benjamin smiled slightly maliciously.

"Why didn't you tell me?"

"Well, pet, I only heard it tonight. I am surprised that you did not already know."

"Why would I keep up with that man? His affairs are of supreme indifference to me." She sniffed, trying desperately to remember what exactly she had said to him.

"Yes, yes, of course. I never thought differently," Mrs. Benjamin concurred with a suspicious tone in her voice. It was very nearly, but not quite, sarcasm. "I know that he has taken a house on Park Lane. Perhaps his sisters will join him there, though I expect he means to fill it with a wife soon enough." Madeline saw her sharp glance. "It is a pity you are so indifferent to him," she continued slyly.

"Quite indifferent," her charge restated firmly.

"And when you used to rub along so well!"

"No, we didn't. We fought all the time!" Madeline returned pettishly, knowing that Mrs. Benjamin had witnessed several of these tiffs.

"Well, that was something else entirely," she replied. She sat for a moment, waiting to be asked what she meant by that, then volunteered, "That was squabbling of people who like each other very well. Very well, indeed." There was still no reply from the opposite seat. "We were beginning to think we were going to have to worry," she continued cryptically.

"About what?" Madeline was finally goaded into asking.

"He is a very good, honorable man, and he obviously admired you very much. He would not have been a bad match for you." Madeline was conscious of a piercing joy upon hearing that he admired her. This was followed immediately by a recollection of his expression tonight. It could not have said more clearly that he despised her and would be delighted to never see her again. She could not think about that.

"Benny! How can you say that! He would have been a bad match for me. All my life I have been taught that some men are eligible and some are not. You remember when I contracted a tendre for the Maths teacher at school and the—"

"He was married."

"Well, yes, but there was also Papa's solicitor."

"He was fifty!"

"No, I mean his clerk. The one with the blue eyes."

"Oh, yes. Well, he was definitely not the kind of man you would marry."

"Why not?"

"Oh, Madeline, you know how these things are. He was not Quality." This seemed to settle the question for Mrs. Benjamin who leaned back onto the squabs with some satisfaction.

"But Mr. Forth had no money to speak of and virtually no family connections. Papa would not have let me marry a tutor!"

Mrs. Benjamin had to think about this comment for a while. "He was well born. He was educated. You know, of course, that unfashionable though it may be, your father wants you to marry someone who will make you happy. He loved your mother very much and would settle on no less for you."

It was Madeline's turn to be silent. "Well, it does not matter if Mr. Forth, or Lord Somerton, or whoever he calls himself now, would have been a good match for me or not," she said at last. "He is a dreadful man, and I don't want to speak of him." Her voice quavered at the end, and she clenched her teeth together to keep from bursting out in a childlike bawl and flinging herself into Mrs. Benjamin's arms to be comforted.

* * *

The next day, it seemed as if there were no respite from the paragon, Lord Somerton. Her three callers, the two Misses Thompson and Miss Chandler were speaking of him the moment they entered the parlor.

"I saw the new Lord Somerton last night." Frances tittered as she accepted a cup of tea. "He is quite handsome. I think it was terribly clever of him to appear late in the season to make a stir just when we were getting tired of all our old beaux." She laughed again.

"Mary danced with him, didn't you, Mary?" Geraldine elbowed her sister to encourage her to give all the details.

"He dances divinely." Mary looked mistily at the ceiling.

"How are things coming with Lord Erickson? Have you brought him up to scratch yet?" Madeline asked suddenly, desperate to turn the topic of conversation away from Forth.

"My, you do use such cant talk, Madeline! You must have picked it up during your rustication," Frances replied with a honeyed smile. "I don't know if I intend to marry Lord Erickson after all. I think Lord Somerton is so much better looking. Besides, it couldn't hurt to shake up Lord Erickson a bit by getting another admirer."

Madeline could not imagine a more annoying laugh than the trill of Frances Chandler.

"I don't know how you intend to catch him, he didn't even look at you last night, Frances." Geraldine lacked Frances's malicious tongue, but she also appeared to lack any semblance of tact.

"That is because I was always dancing with someone else," Frances replied tartly. "He glanced at me several times. And with a very . . . interested expression." She cocked an eyebrow meaningfully. Madeline tried to sink into the cushions of the yellow- and cream-striped sofa, while she waited for the conversation to turn to who was seen dancing with whom, the Peninsular war, or a new bonnet, or the price of potatoes. Anything!

"You danced with him, too." Mary stated suddenly, looking at Madeline. "And you talked quite a while with him. I saw you." Mary managed to look surprised and dewy-eyed no matter what she was saying.

"Well?" both Frances and Geraldine pounced upon her.

"He . . . I . . . we . . . we are actually distantly related. Through marriage." She was surprised that this thought had never really occurred to her before.

"Oooooh." Mary rolled her eyes upward again. "How lucky. You will see him often."

Madeline frowned. If only that were true! Although the way things stood last night, she was not sure the idea held so very much appeal. "I would much rather see more of"—here she grasped desperately for a name—"Lord Stedtson," she declared at random. That started them off.

"Lord Stedtson? Oh, but he is so terribly old!"

"And so rude!"

"And he gambles!" Madeline watched, pleased that the conversation was now racing in three directions at once, directly away from Lord Somerton.

At last the catty trio left, and Madeline was digging into the sofa cushions for the rather thrilling novel she had hastily hidden when her visitors had arrived when the butler intoned the arrival of another visitor. Her heart dropped as he announced Sir George, and she was forced to admit to herself that she had been waiting all day, hoping against reason that Mr. Forth, or Lord Somerton as she would now have to remember to address him, would call. Sir George entered, visibly uncomfortable, but as, until recently, that was his usual state around her, she did not take much notice. Mrs. Benjamin, who had sat in the corner placidly doing her embroidery during the last visit, now perked up and nodded cheerfully at him.

Madeline felt like screaming. She was sick to death of visitors and beaux and stupid flowers and dances and conversations so trite you could go completely deaf and still make the proper replies at the proper times. She wanted nothing more than to go and hide in her old nursery and live off biscuits and milk that Mrs. Benjamin shoved under the door. She wanted to go away to the continent. Anywhere but here in the same town with that man who despised her for some terribly inexplicable reason.

"Miss Delaney, I hope the afternoon finds you well."

"Yes, Sir George, very well. And yourself?"

"Very well, indeed."

"Will you have a cup of tea?"

"Thank you, I will." He sat down. "The weather certainly holds fine for us, doesn't it?" he said, right on schedule.

"It certainly does. Very fine for this time of year." Madeline managed a smile "Do you take cream?"

"No, no, only sugar." This was the point in the conversation where the speaker had several choices: last night's party, tonight's party, someone else's health, or someone else's private life. He unexpectedly chose none of them. "Miss Delaney, I must talk to you," he said suddenly, in a low desperate voice, as if their previous conversation had not signified as talking.

"Do go on, Sir George. I trust Mrs. Benjamin may stay." Madeline's interest was piqued, but she was forced to wait while Sir George turned red.

"Miss Delaney, you spoke to me the other night about you and me . . . you and me being friends."

"Yes."

"You. . . . you do not feel affection toward me beyond what is friendship?" He looked anxious, and Madeline began to feel uncomfortable.

"I care for you very much. However, I do not think that we would make a good match of it. I am sorry, but I cannot return your regard." She smiled tentatively at him, hoping that he understood. Now that she herself had been led on and then spurned, she felt terribly guilty for having done so to him. She felt they shared similar disappointments and so were somewhat kindred. To her surprise, Sir George looked vastly relieved at her little speech.

"I am glad we are friends. You see, I would hate to be thought fickle, and I would certainly never want to pain you. . . ." He seemed to be leading her somewhere in the conversation, but never getting there. Madeline finally grasped what he was saying.

"You are going to propose to Isabella, and you want to make sure that it will not hurt my feelings," she stated triumphantly.

"By Jove, you are one for getting to the heart of things. That is exactly what I was meaning to say. Only you said it much better of course." He slapped his hands on his knees as if this were a great joke.

"I can't believe that you are asking my permission even before asking her father's!" She laughed too. "Of course I do not mind. I have always thought you were well suited to each other. Isabella is a lovely girl, and I have known her this age and think you could truly do no better. I feel certain she will be amenable to your suit." She was more than sure of that, but it would not be right to reveal Isabella's feelings for him.

She was very happy for them. Really, she was. Only her own selfishness was rankled that Sir George, never even a real contender for her affections, should come to her and ask her permission to court her best friend. There were certainly some men who had no compunction about being fickle and changing moods like a weather vane. She really must think of some fine cutting things to say when Lord Somerton spoke to her next. If he ever spoke to her . . .

"I think perhaps the India mulled muslin with the violet ribbons," Madeline said at last. "No . . . well, perhaps the gold and bronze crepe? I can't think today. Which do you think is more becoming?"

"I'm sure I don't know, miss. They are both very beautiful," her maid replied hesitantly.

"Yes, yes, but which makes *me* look more beautiful?" she demanded crossly. At the frightened look of the girl, Madeline instantly repented. "I'm sorry, Letty, I just particularly wanted to be in looks today." She plumped down on her dressing table stool and began to drag a hairbrush savagely through her curls.

"You said that yesterday, too. And the day before."

Madeline's mouth tightened. "So I did." She stared into the grate with a scowl for a moment and then came to a decision. "I am a fool."

"Beg pardon, miss?"

"I am a fool, and I don't care what I wear, so just bring down anything you like for me. And will you be so good as to inform Metworth that I am not at home to him, even if he does call."

"Who, miss?" Letty's eyes were growing rounder as her mistress was showing every sign of having at least a crisis of the nerves if not a full-blown attack of madness.

"Somerton," Madeline replied, in a surprised tone. She leapt up from the stool and began to roam the room with an abstracted air. Letty hesitated in the doorway. "Somerton. He didn't call yesterday when I stepped out to buy some embroidery thread, did he?"

"No, miss." She had answered this question for the fourth time. "I'm sorry."

"Sorry! Don't be sorry. I wouldn't have seen him if he did call. I would have been very angry if he had called, and I am glad that he had the sense to respect my wishes and stay away!"

Letty left the room, concealing an expression of pity, and Madeline continued her pacing. Before she had had a chance to formulate a plan, she heard the knocker fall on the door. Checking the clock on the mantel, she realized that it was too early for a fashionable call, but could not resist running to the spare room which afforded an oblique view of the front door. She was rewarded only with an empty doorstep and the sound of the door closing. She raced back into her room and attempted to put some order to her disheveled hair.

Letty entered with an apologetic air. "Metworth says that Miss Isabella Heresford is here to see you.

I have brought the jonquil muslin, will that suit you?"

"Oh. Of course. Yes, I will see her right away." Madeline's fluttering hands stilled, and she submitted obediently to having her hair dressed.

When she entered the drawing room a few minutes later, she appeared composed and cheerful. Isabella, since she had received Madeline's blessing on her match with Sir George, was in high spirits. She had, in fact, become most irritating company, as she was incessantly, bloomingly happy.

"Are you ready to go to the library? You sent a note around yesterday, saying that you wanted to find a copy of *Childe Harold's Pilgrimage*. I hope there is one to be had. It is still hard to find for all that it came out nearly three months ago. It was published in March just before you left. I have read the first two cantos seven times, and I am desperate for the next one to be published. Sir George and I often read it together. Do you think that he, Childe Harold, I mean, not Sir George of course, will ever find happiness? Sir George says—"

"Don't spoil it for me," Madeline interrupted. "It is all everyone talks of. I declare I know whole sections of it by heart, and I have never even set eyes on the thing!" She laughed and led the way downstairs.

"I suppose you have heard all of the scandalous things that are said about Caro Lamb?" Isabella asked, her voice hushed in awe.

"She and Lord Byron? Yes, it is shocking the way she throws herself at him. It is said that the affair is falling apart, though I saw them together at the Chandlers' musicale the other evening. He was throwing looks at Mary Thompson who, of course, was absolutely delirious with love, though her father would never countenance that match. I hear that his estates are quite encumbered. I was quite embarrassed for Caro. She was quite out of temper and foolish enough to show it. Of course, Lord Byron himself is—"

"So romantic-looking," Isabella finished. "Sir George says he is quite worried that I will cast him off and throw myself at any moppet-headed poet who comes along!" She giggled.

Madeline made a noise of contempt. "I wouldn't throw myself at any man," she declared stoutly. She thought for a moment. "I hear that Frances Chandler has quite thrown her cap over the windmill for Lord—who is he?—Lord Somerton."

"Oh, indeed she has. But he has proved elusive. The musicale was thrown in the hopes that he would come, but he prefers the Corinthian crowd. I don't believe he ever goes to Almack's, but spends all of his time at White's or Watier's or some other gentleman's club. It is really a pity, because it is said that he is a good catch. But, Madeline, I heard you are related to him by marriage or some such thing. How nice that you have already been introduced."

"I suppose," Madeline replied with a careful

shrug. "I myself find that I cannot be fond of him." Isabella also shrugged at this cold pronouncement and appeared to drop the conversation. "Do you know if he will attend the Rochesters' ball?" Madeline asked suddenly.

"Oh, I wouldn't know. I suppose he might. It is one of the biggest events of the season. Sir George says it heralds the beginning of the end of the season. It is a very special night. The Rochesters always go to such trouble to make their ball romantic, with little secret bowers and the funny little lovers' tokens to find. Of course it is all very properly chaperoned. Not a bit improper."

"Bella, how would you know all of this? You have never been there. This is your first season."

"Sir George told me all about it. He says he thinks I shall adore it!" She hugged herself and did a little dance. Madeline could not help laughing at her.

Madeline dressed carefully for the ball and was pleased with the effect. Mrs. Benjamin had frowned when she had picked the icy green silk, since she was of the opinion that young ladies in their first season should not deviate from the white that was practically *de rigeur*. The dress was simple with fine blond lace edging the square neckline. The darker green ribbons and trim, to which Mrs. Benjamin had at last conceded, added a touch of sophistication. The color was unusual and made her blue eyes take on a slightly greener color. She looked poised and calm, neither of which she particularly felt. When Mrs. Benjamin came to dress her hair, she found her standing in the center of the room, staring blankly at her reflection in the mirror.

"What are you wearing such a face for, pet? On such an exciting night?" Mrs. Benjamin's brows went up, her expression almost frightened. Madeline quickly returned from her reverie and smiled.

"I am sorry, Benny; I was woolgathering." Madeline sighed and sat down heavily at the dressing table while Mrs. Benjamin clucked over her. There were times when she stepped back from her own life and wondered if the time at Elmhurst had not been imagined. For the millionth time she played out the scene in the grove when Devin had kissed her. But every time she did this, it seemed to become slightly less real, and she began to wonder if perhaps the scene had only come from the pages of a novel and her own overactive imagination.

Twelve

By the time the carriage arrived at the steps of the Rochester home, Madeline was feeling sick from nervousness. Mrs. Benjamin eyed her suspiciously, but said nothing. Once they entered the ballroom, however, she was entirely distracted by its miraculous transformation. The very large ballroom was now filled with potted trees. A section had been left open for dancing and had been decorated to resemble a woodland glade. Lady Rochester admitted later that she had wanted to carpet the glade with real turf, but had been induced to abandon this idea for technical reasons. Profusions of blooms banked the glade, and the trees surrounding it were arranged to form paths throughout the rest of the room with occasional benches provided, just as in an outdoor garden.

The orchestra was further hidden by foliage which gave the eerie, yet pleasing effect that the music was produced by supernatural means. The chandeliers had been lit with only half their requisite number of candles, which made the room a romantic twilight. Lady Rochester's crowning touch, however, was the lake. On the opposite side of the room from the dance floor and the orchestra, an enormous tub, much like those originally used for crushing grapes, had been filled with water. It was banked with sod and flowers so that it did not look quite so artificial, and on its surface floated water lilies and candles in shallow dishes. Lady Rochester had wanted swans, but her husband had vetoed that idea immediately after its conception.

The entire room had been transformed into a glittering fairyland. Of course this transformation left substantially less room for guests, and they were forced to spill out into the adjoining reception room and onto the balcony which were both decorated in a similar, though less splendid manner. Madeline stood for a moment, stunned, at this transformation of the indoors into the outdoors. Gathering her composure, she descended the stairs with Mrs. Benjamin.

Mrs. Benjamin had at first frowned on the idea of these semisecluded paths through the "woods," but Lady Rochester had cunningly hired young boys and girls from the theater to come and play in the woods dressed as satyrs and wood nymphs. These were given license to play all manner of tricks on any couple so unwitting as to venture to be indiscreet in some secluded grove.

Not entirely mollified, nor should she have been if she had known how easy it was to bribe these "guardians," Mrs. Benjamin enjoined Madeline not to let herself be escorted to the paths for longer than the space of one dance and not to sit down on any of the secluded benches, but to come and sit with her in the open seating if she wished to rest. Feeling very much like little Red Riding Hood being warned against the dangers of the forest, Madeline agreed and then was swept away to join the reel set that was forming in the glade. The magical atmosphere did wonders to lift her spirits, and she felt almost happy as she danced.

It wasn't until the beginning of the third set that she saw Devin. Until then she had not forgotten him, but she at least had been able to pretend he did not exist. She had at least been able to swallow. He had on his arm the exquisite young widow, Lady Champhill. Tall and dark, with the most enviously fine complexion, she embodied the sophistication and Town bronze that Madeline knew she herself did not possess. Compared to her, Madeline was a gawky and overawed greenhorn. Lady Champhill was, indeed, working her magic tonight. She sparkled like her diamonds as she laughed at Devin, and he appeared to glow in her company.

Madeline's first impulse was to run and hide in the woods or in one of the upstairs rooms, but she had done that last time he had appeared and she was determined not to be a coward. Not that he had appeared to notice her presence, she thought with a grimace. Turning almost fiercely with a swirl of blond lace and green ribbons, she smiled dazzlingly upon Lord Quinton who was partnering her at the time. Slightly taken aback, at this unprecedented show of attention, he returned her smile with warmth and squeezed her hand slightly in the next revolution of the dance.

The next few hours were like some ludicrous pantomime. Every time Devin laughed she laughed louder at some witticism of her partner. When he danced, she danced, and it was as many times as allowed with Lord Quinton. She begged him to let someone else get punch for her so that he would not have to leave her side. She knew it was horrid to lead Lord Quinton on like that, but she felt as though she would sink into the ground with shame if Lord Somerton were to know how she mooned over him. Only once did their eyes meet, and she quickly looked away and schooled her features into bland amusement.

Somerton led Lady Champhill in to dinner and sat her down beneath the blooming orange tree that formed the splendid focal point of the dining room before he went to fill her plate from the buffet. Madeline wanted nothing more than to sit as far away from the happy couple as possible. Of course, her partner, Mr. Marks, made a special effort to secure the best seat in the room for her—under the orange tree. As the two ladies had not been formally introduced and Lady Champhill kept company with a much faster circle than she herself did, both women sat stiffly and silently as they waited for their escorts.

Devin's face showed only the slightest flicker of surprise and then shuttered again. He gave her a scant bow before turning his attention to Lady Champhill.

"I do hope you like roast beef. It looked as though it was very good."

"Oh, dear me, I don't think I could eat a bite. Do sit down here beside me. I shall get the most awful crick in my neck from looking up at you." The widow laughed brightly.

"Indeed, I shall. I shall make sure you eat a bit of everything on your plate, just like your old nursey. I won't have you fainting on me later from weakness."

Madeline felt absolutely ill.

"Ah, Somerton. I haven't seen you in a while. How are those grays working out for you?" Mr. Marks sat down with the group.

"They are prime pieces of blood indeed. I owe my F.H.C. membership entirely to them."

"Are you a member of the Four in Hand Club? How very dashing!" Lady Champhill exclaimed, laying her hand on Devin's arm. "How I would love to see you drive. I hear that driving with four horses requires a good deal of skill. But then, I am sure you are skilled in everything."

She lowered her voice with her lashes, but Madeline could clearly hear the innuendo in her words. Her teeth began to ache from clenching her jaw.

"Miss Delaney, you have not eaten a bite! Do not tell me that I have chosen all of the foods you detest!" Mr. Marks cried in dismay.

"Of course not. You have picked everything out

perfectly. How very lavish it all is. Lady Rochester must have gone to a good deal of trouble. So many of these things are not in season." Madeline began a cheerful pretense of eating.

"Indeed, I believe she imported oranges from Spain just for this ball," Somerton commented.

"They are quite too pretty to eat." Madeline took one from the centerpiece on their small table and examined it.

"Yes, it is a pity that she chose to gild some of the fruit. It is so unnecessary when they are so naturally beautiful," he replied pleasantly.

Madeline did not mean to look at him, but her eyes caught with his and she felt a painful surge of desire. She dropped her eyes to her plate.

"I think it looks simply opulent," Lady Champhill said. "I should like to give a dinner party where everything was gilt. Just think, I could serve turtle soup in gilt turtle bowls and gilt lobster and gilt plovers' eggs in aspic and a great gilt pudding!" She laughed her delightful laugh, and all of the gentlemen joined her.

"I declare, Arabella, you would gild ices if you could," Devin teased.

Madeline felt her heart fall within her.

After an interminable time at supper, she returned to the ballroom and sat for a while with Mrs. Benjamin. She longed to see the rest of the forest Lady Rochester had created, but did not really want to be escorted there by a gentleman and would be slightly embarrassed to tour it with her duenna. Isabella would have been a good companion if she had been anywhere in sight. She happened to see Lord Somerton dancing with the hostess's daughter, but it was not as though she had been looking for him.

"Benny darling, I simply must run up and repin my hair," she announced suddenly.

"Let's go up to the ladies withdrawing room, and I will help you." Her duenna turned reluctantly from an old friend she was conversing with.

"No, don't bother coming with me. I shall get the attendant to help me." Amelia waved Mrs. Benjamin back into her seat and headed in the direction of the stairs. When she knew she was out of sight, she then doubled back and entered the wooded path. The trees selected were of different heights so that, in their tubs, some towered over her head. Mrs. Benjamin needn't have worried about anything scandalous happening in the trees as they were absolutely teeming with people. Madeline wandered down the winding paths made by the trees, trying not to feel foolish that she was unescorted.

Some might have deemed the lake a disappointment. It was really no more than a small pond, but the effect, with the light from the chandeliers sparkling off the water, was really quite spectacular. The orchestra sounded more muffled here through the trees, and the ungainly satyrs and wood nymphs were raucously chasing each other around the pool. Madeline wished she could have a moment alone in the twilight fairyland, but contented herself with sitting on one of the flower-bedecked benches beside the pool. She rested her forehead briefly against its cool iron back and tuned out the squealing laughter of the revelers. She felt a sudden gust of wind pass over her hair and looked up. Lord Somerton had swatted away the menacing hand of a young satyr who bounded off out the balcony doors.

"He was about to dunk your hair ribbons," he explained gravely.

"Oh," Madeline replied, swallowing hard to try to force her heart back down into her chest. With annoyance, she realized that she was blushing and refused to look at him. "It is nice to see you again, Mr.—Lord Somerton." At being met with silence, she at last raised her head and saw that he was regarding her intently. She knew, too late, that her expression had been one of frustrated longing. To her surprise, after a moment, his own features relaxed and he smiled, slightly, but naturally.

"You are looking well."

"Thank you." Madeline's voice sounded breathless to her own ears, and she resisted the temptation to squirm under the compliment. "My lord, I must tell you that I had no idea you . . . you had inherited a title." She felt her face grow warmer. "I hope I did not sound rude to you when we last met. I was simply surprised to see you. Surprised and pleased," she added, again unable to look at him. She sensed that he sat down next to her.

"You have grown shy, Miss Delaney." He laughed softly. "You hardly seem the harum-scarum girl I remember."

"It has been quite a long time since I have seen you," she replied, careful to avoid sounding accusatory.

"Yes, too long. I must apologize for my precipitous departure from Elmhurst. I am sure you have heard by now that there was a sudden death in my family." He made a move, as though he were about to take her hand, but thought better of it. "That is a frail excuse, however. I should have told you myself that I was leaving. I am afraid I was rather cowardly. There was much unfinished business between us." He smiled. His gray eyes had much more of a shade of green about them than she remembered, and she felt herself leaning unconsciously leaning toward them, mesmerized.

"I am sorry for your loss," Madeline murmured. She noticed that his hand, the one that had been so close to touching hers, now toyed absently with a bit of ribbon on his watch chain. "That is mine," she said, catching hold of it. "That was my bookmark that day in the parlor."

"It is." He sat silently, looking at her for a moment. "Madeline—" he began, an expression of anguish crossing his face, "I have wanted so much to speak with you."

She leaned closer.

"The day I left Elmhurst . . . I . . ." His voice trailed off.

She realized that she was still holding the ribbon

on his watch chain. He covered her fingers with his own. "Please . . ." He knew what she was asking, and he closed the space between them. Madeline drew her breath in sharply.

"Lord Somerton! There you are! How cruel of you to abandon me!" Lady Champhill called out archly. "Oh, but I see you are fickle and have found someone else to amuse you. Never mind. I am sure that Lord Quinton can escort me home, since both he and I have been rejected." She laughed brittlely and patted that man on the arm.

Devin rose languidly to his feet. "Lady Champhill, forgive me. I had not forgotten about you at all. I would be happy to escort you home if you are ready for your carriage to be called. I did not know that you were waiting."

"Oh, please do not let me disturb your little tête-à-tête," she protested with elaborate gestures.

Madeline was forced to master her irritation as Lord Quinton swooped down upon her and immediately bore her off toward the front of the room.

Lady Champhill smiled brightly at Devin. "Has she run you to ground at last? The girl has been staring at us all night." Her eyes followed Madeline's retreating form. "I daresay you were only being kind to her, but I would hate for anyone to be led astray by Miss Delaney."

"What do you mean?" he demanded darkly.

"Well, I myself have always championed her, but there are some who are not quite so charitable about . . ." Her voice trailed off modestly.

"What?"

"Well, she is thought, by some extremely high sticklers, mind you, to be just the slightest bit . . . fast." Lady Champhill squeezed his arm. "I have always thought it was just high spirits myself, but she is *quite* vivacious, and some young men have perhaps taken it in the wrong way. You would think she would have learned . . . especially after the Incident. . . ." She looked up at Devin with wide hazel eyes. "But of course you knew about that."

"I knew," Devin replied quietly.

"I never agreed with people who said that she brought it on herself. Her duenna should have kept her away from Lambrook, of course. It would have been much better for her reputation, though, if she had been a little more circumspect once she returned from her . . . country visit."

She sighed and shook her head. "One has to be so careful as a debutante." She again raised her heavily fringed eyes to him. "Of course, as a widow, I have so much more freedom."

"Indeed," he said grimly.

She watched him closely. "I have even heard that she has spoken about you."

Devin turned to her with an expression of surprise.

"She brags that she has kept you dangling and will bring you up to scratch by the end of the season," Arabella continued on without noticing. "She claims that she will have had an offer from nearly every eligible peer of the realm. Of course that is not possibly true, since she is regarded by most as damaged goods. Society can be so cruel, and girls can be so foolish." She sighed again and then lifted her lovely white shoulders. "But she is young and is testing her powers. We must forgive young people their foibles."

"Of course"—his expression was impassive—"but enough about Miss Delaney."

"Yes, indeed. Enough about Miss Delaney." Lady Champhill smiled sweetly.

Thirteen

"Isabella, I need your help." Madeline strode into the drawing room with a determined air. She carried with her a slim leather case, which she proceeded to open. She then spread its contents on the occasional table: a large ream of foolscap, various implements for writing, two of Mrs. Radcliffe's novels, the copy of *Childe Harold* which she had forgotten to return to the lending library, a map of London, a leather purse full of coins, and an orange.

"With what?" Her friend looked wary as she observed the signs that Madeline was hatching a plot which would invariably end in disaster.

"I am in love."

"Oh, dear. Again?"

Madeline shot her a withering look. "This is the real thing, Bella, so there is no need to be sarcastic."

"I wasn't," Isabella replied in confusion. She gave a short laugh and set down her needlework. "All right, Madeline, tell me all about it."

She hesitated a moment. "It is Lord Somerton."

"What?" Isabella's brows flew up. "I did not even know that you knew him."

"He . . . I . . . I met him at Elmhurst." A blush crept up her cheeks as she recalled their last meeting there. "I simply must get him to marry me," she stated firmly, shaking off the tingling warmth that darted through her.

"Very well," Isabella replied calmly. "How do you propose to go about it."

"Well"—Madeline drew out the syllable, her expression perplexed—"it is difficult because I am not at all sure that he does not despise me." She stared into space for a moment. "I always seem to make him very angry, and nearly every conversation we have ends in a quarrel. He is a very high stickler for propriety and quite the most arrogant man I have ever met."

"I cannot see why you would want to marry him then," Isabella remarked, taking up her needlework again.

"I don't either, but I do." She made an impatient gesture. "Regardless, I do think there is some hope. In fact, things were going well last night at the Rochesters' ball until Lady Champhill interrupted us." She wrinkled her nose at the name.

"Perhaps you should engineer another opportunity."

"Should I write him a letter?" Madeline sat bolt upright and haphazardly began collecting her writing tools, "I could tell him that I love him and then—"

"Good heavens, no!" Isabella protested in horror. "What would your father say? Writing a gentleman . . . well, it is too brazen by half. You would do much better to employ a little subtlety."

"Subtlety? Or subterfuge?" Madeline gave a wry laugh. "You are right, of course. It is just that I am slightly at a loss. . . ." She twisted a fallen strand of hair around her finger and pondered.

"You said he was a high stickler. Perhaps if you acted with a little more . . ." Isabella let the words hang suggestively.

"Yes, yes, act a little more circumspectly. But then again, he seems to have a definite preference for Lady Champhill."

Isabella rolled her eyes. "Hardly circumspect."

They sat silence for a moment.

"I suppose I shall just have to act more like her," Madeline said resignedly at last.

Isabella grimaced. "I think it would be much better if you were to behave more as he would wish you to."

"Oh, pooh! And be so boring? He only thinks he wants someone prim and proper. If he really did, he wouldn't be courting Lady Champhill. I shall out-Champhill her." She again pulled the paper to her and began cutting her quill with more energy than skill.

"What are you doing?"

"I am writing out ideas of things to say, and we will practice them so that I do not forget them when the time comes." She began writing furiously, pausing at intervals to think. "You shall ask your mama if we may plan an outing, say, to the Royal Gallery or to the Elgin Marbles. And you will make sure that you invite Lord Somerton."

"But I hardly know him!" Isabella protested.

"But your mother does. I saw them speaking the evening of the Rochesters' ball. And"—Madeline arched an eyebrow—"he has become great friends with Sir George. It is natural that you should invite him. We shall make sure it is a large party so that he will not get suspicious."

"I suppose so," Isabella agreed reluctantly. "As long as Mama and Mrs. Benjamin will chaperone."

"Oh, dear, not Mrs. Benjamin! Then he will certainly know that something is afoot. Perhaps your aunt Fanny or your sister Lady Windon will oblige us. I would not like Lord Somerton to know that I was involved in the planning of this."

"As you wish. But please do not expect me to do anything. I do not like playacting. I would simply die from nervousness."

"No, no. You will not have to do a thing but enjoy yourself. Once we are there, I shall be on my best behavior. I will flirt with no one else but him, so that he does not think he is merely one of several men I admire." She began writing furiously. "I shall remark that I am jealous of Lady Champhill."

"Oh, Madeline, you wouldn't!"

"But I shall! If I say it like this: 'I am simply *madly* jealous of Lady Champhill!'" She demonstrated the sentence with a teasing smile and a look from the corners of her eyes and then continued in her normal voice, "He will know that I am not serious, but perhaps will hope that I am a little serious."

"You missed your calling, Madeline. You should tread the boards." Isabella laughed.

"And then I will say 'I was *terribly* disappointed that we were interrupted the evening of the Rochesters' ball. I was *so* looking forward to a tête-à-tête with you.' Don't you think using French is sophisticated?"

"Oh, yes, do use French." Isabella dropped her embroidery and joined her friend on the couch.

"Shall I say a *'petit tête-à-tête'*?"

"Perhaps that is a bit much."

"Then I will remark that it is just a shame we are not such intimates as we were in the country."

"Do not say intimates," Isabella protested. "Only a woman friend can be your intimate."

"Do you think so?"

"Oh, yes. I think saying that you were intimates in the country implies . . . well implies . . ." Isabella's eyebrows went up expressively.

"Oh, dear." Madeline blushed at the highly improper thoughts that gesture spawned. "Perhaps I should say that we were such good friends in the country," she remarked vaguely, still thinking of that morning in the willow grove. His kiss had produced such an agonizing combination of desire and bone-wilting dizziness, her whole body experienced a frisson of energy at the memory.

"Madeline, are you quite all right?" Isabella peered anxiously at her friend.

"Certainly." She pressed a cooling hand to her warm cheeks. "I am fine. I know exactly how things will work out now." She went back to her writing with renewed vigor, liberally consulting both Mrs. Radcliffe and Lord Byron.

"Why did you bring all of these things?" Isabella asked, poking with interest among the contents of Madeline's case.

"Well, you never know what you will need when you have to plan such things," she replied, taking the orange and peeling it while she examined a particularly passionate passage in the second canto.

"Well, I suppose plots do work best when they involve the bringing of men up to scratch," Isabella observed mildly.

The proposed outing did not take place until three days later and was comprised of a group of nine young people of Isabella's acquaintance. They were to go to the Royal Gallery, chaperoned by Isabella's mother and her married sister. Madeline had spent the entire morning changing her gowns in fits of indecision and in rehearsing the various moods and phrases of her flirtation with Lord Somerton. There had been quite a scare when he had not replied immediately to Isabella's invitation, but at last, the affirmative reply came. He would be there.

Madeline had planned to arrive at Isabella's house on Belgrave square late so it would not appear that she had had anything to do with the planning of the outing, and so she was not in the drawing room when he arrived.

As she was shown up to the drawing room, she forced herself to slow her breathing and smoothed her face into a neutral expression. She felt as though she were about to go on stage. Her heart fell as she entered the room and scanned it over Isabella's shoulder as she offered her cheek for a kiss from her friend. He had not arrived. Just as she moved away, she saw Isabella's expression change to a guilty blush and knew before she turned around that he had arrived right on her heels. Poor Isabella, blushing and stammering as she greeted him, making lame, ridiculous excuses as to why she'd invited him when none were necessary. Madeline cringed.

Happily, Sir George was quickly at Isabella's side and offered to make the introductions. Madeline pretended to be listening to the prattling of Frances while she carefully observed the new arrival. He looked so much fiercer than he had at Elmhurst. His straight dark brows were drawn together in a slight frown as he bowed over the hand of one of the Misses Thompson and made the requisite comments. The gray-green of his eyes was pale and unreadable. Madeline hoped the heavy, sudden beating of her heart and the unprecedented weakness she felt would pass, and was seized with the agonizing certainty that she had worn the entirely wrong ensemble altogether. Controlling the urge to flee the room, she managed to smile when Sir George brought Lord Somerton around to where she sat.

"You are acquainted with Lord Somerton, are you not, Miss Delaney?"

He took her hand and bowed over it. "Yes, of course."

She tried to make her smile warm rather than nervous and was glad the gloves she wore disguised the fact that not only were her hands trembling, but they had suddenly developed the most unladylike tendency to perspire as well. He took her hand and bowed over it. Madeline tried to see his expression, but it was as carefully blank as her own. As Lord Somerton was the last to arrive, the party began to take up their wraps and move downstairs to where Isabella's mama and Lady Windon had provided their landeaus for the outing.

It was Isabella's brother Robert who escorted her down the stairs while Lord Somerton took the arm of one of the lucky Misses Thompson. She managed to be sorted into the same landeau as he, but he resolutely refused to look at her for the entire trip. It was very difficult to keep a calm mien as Frances Chandler was seated at his left and could not seem to refrain from tittering and wildly twirling her parasol. Madeline mentally rehearsed her lines and bided her time.

The gallery presentation was quite spectacular, and it was quite some time before she realized that she was missing her chance. Lord Somerton had not approached her all afternoon. Lord Innings, however, had spent three-quarters of an hour cajoling and teasing her to no effect. Annoyed with her monosyllabic replies, he had turned his attentions to the more receptive Miss Chandler. This left Somerton free from a conversation partner for the first time that day, so Madeline quickened her steps to walk with him. She drew a breath and brightened her smile in preparation to launching into her witty banter even as she suddenly experienced misgivings as to the wisdom of this course.

"Miss Delaney, I do not appreciate your scheming," he said sternly before she had even begun. Madeline was so taken by surprise that she could not reply. "It was your doing that I should be invited on this outing," he continued.

"Yes, it was." She had recovered enough to sound pert. "I was so *very* disappointed that we were interrupted when I last spoke to you. I was so looking forward to a little tête-à-tête." She paused and looked at him coquettishly. His brows rose slightly, but he did not respond. "Lady Champhill interrupted us as you recall. I'm simply *wildly* jealous of her, you know."

"Wildly jealous," he echoed with a humorless smile. Madeline plunged on intrepidly.

"She has quite taken you away from me. I thought we were on such good terms at Elmhurst." She smiled so that her dimple showed and wished she had brought a fan to flutter. She was delighted when he stopped walking and allowed the group ahead of them to continue on.

"Miss Delaney"—he turned quickly on his heel to face her, looking down into her face with such an intent expression that her pulse began to race again—"do you ever stop?"

"Do I ever stop?" This was not what she had expected to hear.

"I met a woman in the country whom I grew to respect for her sincerity when she wasn't acting like a fool. Here in London, you seem to have entirely lost the ability to converse in a normal manner."

"Devin . . . Mr. For— My lord, I . . ."

"I dislike your extremely unladylike manner of soliciting my attention." His jaw was set stiffly, and his eyes were as cool as water.

Madeline felt the blood rise to her face. "I do beg your pardon," she said acidly. "I had forgotten just how annoyingly pompous you are. I must remember to write these things down." She smiled sweetly.

"Do try to remember to show some good breeding, my dear. You do not seem to care for your reputation, but I prefer not to torch mine by being seen in a shouting match with you."

"Who is shouting?" Madeline hissed. "I am simply stating facts."

"As was I. Your father should have horse-whipped some manners into you years ago." His tone was mild, but there was a tremor of fury in it.

Madeline clenched her fists. "You were over-bearing and prudish as Mr. Forth, but now that you are someone of consequence, you think you must look down your nose at everyone. You are hardly a gentleman." She saw his face pale and knew that she had drawn blood. She instantly felt ashamed, but only pressed her lips together and regarded him defiantly.

"I will refrain from commenting in kind, Miss Delaney," he said softly at last. "Please allow me to remove myself from your company." He left her where she stood and went to join the others.

"Oh, dear," Madeline ruefully said to a large, headless statue of a Roman warrior, "that did not go very well at all."

Fourteen

"All the world seems to be out in the park to-day," Sir George commented cheerfully as he tooled his carriage through the throng.

Isabella smiled and nodded cheerfully to an acquaintance, but turned back to him with an anxious expression. "I am worried."

"No need to be. I may not drive to an inch, but I have never turned this thing over. With a lady in it, I mean."

"No, I mean about Madeline."

"Oh, Miss Delaney." He nodded in understanding.

"There is Sally Jersey. Do wave at her. She was very kind to make sure that I had vouchers for Almack's at the beginning of the season." They bowed at that woman, but were relieved when she showed no disposition to stop her carriage to talk. "Madeline said I could tell you about . . . her plan to marry Lord Somerton, on account of our being engaged now," Isabella continued, smiling fondly up at him, "but you will remember not to say anything, won't you?"

"Of course," he replied with a somewhat injured expression. "But I do hate the idea of the poor man being hunted unwarned."

Isabella frowned at him. "She insists that she must lay these convoluted plans."

"She is a strange one. Too wild by half for me."

"Oh, you didn't used to think so," she teased, slipping her arm possessively through his.

George had the grace to blush. "Don't quiz me, Bella. You know that Miss Delaney would never have suited me. I think she needs someone she cannot run roughshod over."

"Like Lord Somerton," Isabella prompted.

"Perhaps. But he shouldn't be forced into it by some chit's trickery."

"Of course not! It is not as though she were plotting to get him into a compromising situation to force him to propose." The worried wrinkle between her brows reappeared. "At least I do not think so. No, Maddie would never do that. She wants him to love her, not just marry her." She sighed. "I just wish I knew what she will do next."

"By Jove, there she is! I told you all the world is out today. Let's take her up and ask her what she means to do." Madeline had been walking with her maid, feeling rather dispirited about the events of the previous week, and had no objection to being driven around the park.

"But you must not be too loving in front of me," she warned them. "I am delighted with your engagement, but you must not flaunt it in my face." She laughed a little forcedly.

Isabella settled her friend beside her, though the carriage was crowded with three in it, and asked gently after her health.

"Oh, you needn't be so solicitous, Bella! I am not about to go into a decline simply because of a romantic setback! I have other plans up my sleeve!"

"I thought you would." Isabella winced.

"I simply cannot understand what went wrong! It is too unfair! On the night of the Pembroke masquerade, I explained that the last time we had spoken I had not understood that his situation had changed. He was so kind and understanding, and he said we had much to discuss. I thought he was on the verge of kissing me!"

"Madeline!" Isabella looked shocked and turned quickly to see if anyone also driving in the park had heard the scandalous comment.

"Oh!" Madeline exclaimed helplessly. "I felt things were going exceedingly well and then, the outing yesterday was disastrous! He was like a different person. An exceedingly unpleasant person at that. I wonder if I could have mistaken someone else for him at the Pembroke masquerade. . . ."

"I think it is unlikely."

"I cannot imagine what has happened to him, then. He seems to suffer from . . . moods. Perhaps. . . . perhaps Lady Champhill has turned him against me."

"Madeline, you must not assume that everyone puts as much effort into machinations as you do."

Sir George laughed. He had been allowed into Madeline's confidence on account of his engagement to Isabella, but always seemed to play the irksome role of The Voice of Reason in most of her plans.

Madeline sniffed in disdain. "I had worked everything out so carefully, and he was just horrid to me."

"Perhaps you were a bit *too* vivacious?" Isabella suggested gently.

"Obviously," Madeline snapped, but then she was forced to paste on a bright smile as an acquaintance nodded to them from horseback. As soon as the fashionably dressed woman had passed, her face returned to its original scowl. "We were completely wrong. The man cannot stand to be in my presence!" As much as this dramatic statement seemed to require gestures, Madeline kept her hands in her lap and her face composed. She bowed placidly as another group of their friends drove by.

"How terrible!" Isabella also smiled at the passing carriage. She then sighed dramatically. "Your love is destined to remain unrequited."

"Not everyone is going to fall in love with you," George announced cheerfully.

"Bah!" Madeline could not resist flinging her arms up in a gesture of disgust. "If I did not love him so much, I would truly hate that man. I simply must come up with another plan."

"No, Maddie! Please, you will only get yourself

into more of a stew! Let him alone and let's have no more of your plans."

By this time they had both nearly forgotten themselves and their surroundings, and were speaking with such animation that Sir George was forced to clear his throat audibly. They sat in silence for a few moments, smiling and nodding vapidly to others in the park, the ludicrousness of the entire situation then striking them both as so funny that they were reduced to giggles and had to be driven home.

"I was so *very* disappointed that we were interrupted the last time we spoke. I was *so* looking forward to a tête-à-tête with you," Lady Champhill purred.

Devin nearly choked, but managed to recover and hide his grin behind his napkin.

The widow continued. "All these supper dances are such a bore. So many old tabbies watching everything you say and do. I was vastly hoping that you would take me for a turn in the park one of these days. I am so very anxious to see those new grays of yours. What color is your phaeton?"

"A dark gray. Charcoal, I suppose you would call it."

"Marvelous! I have the most wonderful carriage dress that would suit it. It is royal blue. Do you not think that would look very fine?"

"Indeed. Very nice," he replied.

"You are very distracted," she accused, her pretty mouth growing petulant.

"I am sorry. I will make it up to you when we go driving. I shall take you to your next partner. I believe you said it was Marks?" He led her inexorably toward that gentleman.

"Will you dance with me later?"

"I regret that I may not be able to. My friend Garring has recently arrived, up from Somerset, and I should like to devote the rest of the evening to ensuring his amusement here in Town." He bowed over her hand and withdrew to the card room as she turned to Marks with a frustrated twitch of her skirts.

"Ah, so you have extricated yourself from the widow's clutches," Jeremy Garring murmured when Devin appeared at his elbow. "I hope you know that she is panting to get you into the parson's mousetrap." He continued to scrutinize the crowd through a quizzing glass tied to a silk ribbon.

"On the contrary," Devin replied dryly, "she has intimated that no such legal steps would be necessary."

Garring's eyes flickered to Devin's over the glass. He whistled softly. "Can't say even that appeals to me." He lowered his voice even more. "She frightens me. She is quite a beauty, though."

"Indeed." Devin gave a dry laugh. "I am ashamed to say that I use her as a bit of a scarecrow. She keeps the matchmaking mamas away. I think I am aware of her true feelings for me."

"Which are?"

"None."

Garring laughed. "I see someone here who should interest you," he commented, training his glass to the door. He heard a soft curse emanate from the man beside him. "She is quite improved from the long-ago days of Elmhurst, wouldn't you say?"

Devin did not reply. His eyes were fixed on Madeline, descending the stairs in a magnificent cream-colored silk with an overdress of god net. It emphasized her perfect complexion and turned her hair to the gold of a guinea coin. He took a glass of champagne from a passing waiter and turned to make his way to the card room.

"Quite a taking little thing," Jeremy drawled. I thought you had developed a bit of a tendre for her."

"Me?" Devin's brows rose in surprise. "I should hardly think so. She is a child. I have found that there are many more sophisticated ladies in town."

"Ah, yes. A certain dashing widow we shall not mention." Jeremy leered. "Well, I am delighted to hear it. That leaves the lovely Miss Delaney all to myself."

Devin drained the champagne and examined the glass. "You would think they would serve the decent stuff," he murmured. "You are welcome to the manic Miss Delaney," he stated coolly. "I find her tiresome to the extreme."

Garring's brows rose in some surprise, but he

did not question his friend's pronouncement. He put the quizzing glass to his eyes again and then started, "Good God!" he exclaimed. "Lambrook!"

"He is here?"

"Yes, can you believe that he is received? I'd say we know a story or two that would ensure he is blackballed from polite society. Shall we let him know his presence is unwelcome?" Jeremy started across the floor.

Devin caught his sleeve. "Let him be," he commanded, his eyes narrow. "Let's just keep him in our sights."

Madeline felt her stomach drop. There, across the room was Lord Lambrook, looking his usual sartorial self. He leaned easily against a pillar, his dark, hooded eyes assessing everything that went on in the room. He had not seen her yet, but there was no doubt that he would. She quelled the desire to run and forced herself to smile at her dancing partner and walk on trembling legs to the dance floor.

After a few moments, her face felt stiff from smiling. She could not concentrate on the steps of the dances and found herself always looking around for Lord Lambrook. She prayed fervently that whatever Madeline-amnesia he had suffered upon their meeting in Elmhurst would reappear now. She screwed up her courage and looked around while she was moving up the line in a country dance. He was standing in the same place he had been, but was now regarding her intently. She felt dizzy with fear and pretended not to see him.

"Miss Delaney! You have gone pale! You look as though you may faint. Pray let me take you to a seat." Lord Whitton insisted that she break out of the formation of the dance and led her to a settee. Madeline was relieved to note that it was quite a distance from where Lambrook stood. Her partner patted her hand solicitously for a few moments and then announced his intention to get her some lemonade.

"No, please, don't leave! Do not trouble yourself."

"Nonsense, my dear. I will not have you overexerting yourself. You will feel much better once you have had something cool to drink."

Despite repeated protests, Lord Whitton bounded off into the crowd. Madeline looked around apprehensively. From where she sat she could not see the place where Lambrook had been standing. However, as there were many people around her, she relaxed slightly.

"Miss Delaney, it is such a pleasure to see you again." A low familiar voice drawled in her ear.

"Lord Lambrook," she said weakly.

"Now, now, there is no need for you to look so frightened. After all, it was not you and I who quarreled, now was it?" He smiled warmly and sat down beside her. "We always got along very well, and I feel that I must apologize *profusely* for any

misunderstanding there might have been at Elmhurst. You must know that I have always had the
utmost admiration and respect for you." He took
her hand in his. "In fact, I have thought of you
often in the last few months, Miss Delaney."

"Please, Lord Lambrook"—she attempted to
extract her hand—"we should not be having this
conversation."

"I do not mean to distress you. It seems that I
am always swept away in your presence." His eyes
were so dark that they seemed pupil-less in the
candlelight. "Will you meet me in private?"

"No, I will not," Madeline exclaimed in some
surprise.

"Please Miss Delaney, understand it is not that
I wish to press my attentions on you. I am perfectly content to admire you from afar. It is just
that I have some very important news I must give
to you in private."

She regarded him with suspicion. "Then tell me
now."

"No, I cannot. Your partner is returning. Believe
me, it is very important, and you would wish to
hear it in private. I can tell you that it involves a
man you think is your friend, Lord Somerton."

"What?"

"Meet me in the library as soon as you can,"
he commanded. He pressed her hand and then
disappeared into the crowd. Madeline looked
around and suddenly saw Lord Somerton watching her intently from across the room. Their eyes
locked, but he remained entirely expressionless.

"Are you feeling more the thing, Miss Delaney?" Lord Whitton inquired solicitously as he arrived with her punch.

"Yes. Much better. Thank you so much. I feel very silly. If you do not mind, though, I think I will go up to the ladies withdrawing room and lie down with some hartshorn for a moment. Please do not tell Mrs. Benjamin, though. She will only fuss, and I should not like her to worry. I shall be fine in a moment." Smiling, she waved him away and darted down the darkened hallway to the library.

The room was empty when she arrived, but as it was intended to be used as an additional withdrawing room, the door was open and it was well lit. She took a turn around it to assess whether her meeting with Lord Lambrook would be private. As no one lurked in any of the book-filled recesses, she seated herself on one of the jacquard-upholstered sofas. Lambrook entered and smiled when he saw her. Closing the door carefully behind him he crossed the room to her.

"Ah, Miss Delaney, I knew that you would be here." He took her hands in his and gazed at her fondly.

"What is it that you wish to tell me?" she demanded, withdrawing her hands. She clasped them firmly in her lap.

Lambrook seated himself close beside her. "I cannot tell you how happy I was to find you here tonight. I have thought of you night and day since we parted." He leaned closer to her.

"What do you wish to tell me?" she repeated, regretting that she had not asked him to leave the door open.

"I wanted to warn you. I wanted to keep you from harm." He possessed himself of her hand again. "Mr. Forth, who now calls himself Lord Somerton, is nothing but a sham."

"What do you mean?"

"He is nothing but an encroaching nobody who has come into his title by trickery." In response to Madeline's raised brows, he continued. "There is some doubt that his parents were actually married. . . ." He lowered his voice conspiratorially. "I do not want to cause trouble, but this is what I have heard. I wanted you to know before you became too deeply involved with him."

Madeline regarded him coldly. "I thank you for your concern; however, you need not have worried." She attempted to rise, but he restrained her. She shook off his gloved hand on her arm, but remained seated.

"There is something else."

She did not reply, but looked impatient.

"Do not be so cruel, Miss Delaney. You know how long I have waited for you." Madeline made a noise of disbelief. "We have been star-crossed from the start. I realized when I was on the continent, how very much . . . how very much I love you. I love you passionately." He grasped both of her arms and attempted to embrace her. "You must marry me!"

"I believe we have had this conversation before." Madeline pulled back stiffly and looked at him in disgust. And I believe I refused your flattering request."

"Do not be coy, my dear. Surely you have felt the passion that is between us." There was an edge to his voice now that frightened her.

"I can only imagine that you have had an extraordinary run of bad luck at the tables and have an eye on my inheritance." She had spoken somewhat sarcastically, but when his expression revealed surprise for an instant, she knew that it was true. "You wicked fortune hunter!" she exclaimed with a disbelieving laugh.

His fingers tightened painfully on her arms. "Marry me."

The hunted look in his eyes made her afraid, and she began to struggle. Lambrook instantly let her go. She ran to the door, but saw from the gaping keyhole that it was locked.

"Madeline, Madeline. May I call you Madeline now?" He smiled his white-toothed smile and crossed the room to her.

"Tell me what you want." She moved away from him when he approached, her hands held out to ward him off.

He laughed, but his previously affectionate tone was replaced with one that was cold and disinterested. "You are frightened my dear. Never fear, although you are a lovely little piece, I have absolutely no interest in ravishing you. Disappointed?"

She did not reply, but was mentally calculating

how painful it would be to leap from a first-story window.

"You seemed willing enough to damage your reputation at the start of the season," he taunted. "Very indiscreet of you, my dear," he said, shaking his head, "especially when it comes to light that you were even more indiscreet at your aunt and uncle's country estate. And then there was that even more unfortunate incident of the duel. A duel for the honor of a little ruined hussy is quite, quite laughable. Dueling is so passé. It would make you look terribly unacceptable to most hostesses. How disappointed your father will be." He spoke calmly, without menace, but Madeline felt panic rising within her.

"There was no duel. You ran away!" She retreated behind a chair.

"That is not the way I remember it. I wonder who will believe you and who will believe me."

"Do you want money. Is that it? Are you blackmailing me?" Hoping that she was concealed by the chair, she picked up an ornamental brass crocodile from a table.

"I would hardly call it something so vulgar as that. I am simply curious as to what your reputation is worth to you." Lambrook shrugged nonchalantly. "I think ten thousand pounds should not be amiss. I mean, after all, if your reputation is kept sterling, you are likely to make a very good match. It is an infinitesimal price to pay for social acceptance."

"I don't have that kind of money. I could never pay it."

"My dear girl, I hardly expect you to be giving me your pin money. Your father is the one holding the purse strings. I am certain he is willing to bestow a little nothing . . . a vail really, to ensure that his only daughter is free of damaging scandal. I mean really, saddled with such a hoydenish creature as you I would be surprised to learn he has not had to do so several times." He raised his quizzing glass to his eyes and regarded her intently.

Madeline struggled to master her rage. "Then why did you not lock my papa in a room with you, you coward?"

"Good heavens, such language. I really think you will ruin yourself despite my help." He sighed tiredly. "I obviously thought it much more delicate to approach you about this matter than your parent."

"Your threats are useless you know. No one would believe your wild stories. Lord Somerton will corroborate with me." Behind the chair, she tightened her grasp on her weapon.

"Ah, yes, the jumped-up tutor." His black brows rose sarcastically. "Actually my dear"—he crossed the room and wrenched the crocodile out of her grasp in one swift movement as though it had never presented the slightest threat—"perhaps I should remind you that even as we speak, we are here alone in a room. Surely your chaperone is anxious. I could always arrange that someone could see us here together. And I could always arrange it so that your reputation would be very, very compromised."

He shook his head sadly. "Of course, I might have to marry you, but I was prepared to do that. However, if you prove troublesome, I think you would find that marriage to me might be extremely unpleasant for you."

In one swift movement, Madeline grabbed a heavy crystal vase full of flowers and, with both hands, slammed it against his head. He dropped like a stone, covered with peonies and water. "Oh, God!" she gasped, the vase thudding to the floor from her nerveless fingers, "I have killed him."

Fifteen

She ran to the door and pulled desperately at it several times before she remembered that it was locked. Fighting down hysteria, she raced back to Lambrook's prostrate form. She picked up the vase, prepared to use it again if he should be re-animated suddenly while she searched his pockets. She realized in confusion that she was panting and sobbing, but managed to find the key and flee to the door. Opening it, she careened into a broad chest.

"Madeline?" Devin pulled her off him and looked at her. She clutched him as her legs gave way, and she then collapsed into paroxysms of tears. He pushed her back inside the library and shut the door even though she incoherently resisted. She knew he saw Lambrook's body when he jerked in surprise. "What happened?" he demanded urgently. She was utterly unable to reply until she heard a low moan from the corner behind the chair.

"He is not dead! I haven't killed him!" she exclaimed, shaking Devin to make him understand.

The man was maddeningly calm. He disengaged her fists and crossed the room to crouch over Lambrook.

"No, you have not. That shall be quite a lump, though." He stood. "I assume he deserved it."

Madeline could only nod and collapse onto the sofa. Her limbs burned as the panic receded. Lambrook was now attempting to rise, and Devin solicitously helped him to a chair.

"Lord Lambrook, how surprised I am to find you here." He smiled icily. "I hope that you are feeling more the thing."

"You? What the devil are you doing here?" Lambrook squinted at him in confusion.

"I am considering calling you out yet again," Devin replied. "I recall that you had some objections to the propriety of my calling you out when I was merely a tutor. That has happily been rectified, so I could not allow you to miss the opportunity to wake at dawn and attempt to kill me." He pulled Lambrook out of the chair by the lapels, and commanded Madeline to stay where she was with a ferocious frown.

"However," he continued calmly, slinging an arm around the limp man and propelling him forcefully out of the room, "I am sorry to say that I doubt we will have the pleasure, since, much like last time, you will be gone before morning." Lambrook struggled weakly in Devin's grip, but did not reply.

They received several quizzical looks as they made their way down the stairs, but the guests only shook their heads and muttered comments regarding the imprudence of serving champagne punch so early in the evening. "Did you ever do a grand tour, Lambrook?" Devin asked suddenly, in a completely conversational tone as they entered the card room.

"No," Lambrook answered with a sullen scowl.

"I think now would be a good time." He smiled at Jeremy who looked stunned to see Devin's companion. "Jeremy, don't you think that it is a perfect time for Lambrook to make the grand tour."

"I hear Greece is lovely," Jeremy replied mildly, rising up and taking Lambrook's other arm. He guided the trio out the French doors.

"Let go of me!"

"Yes, yes, but I fear the continent is somewhat dangerous, what with Boney romping about. Perhaps you would fancy something more tropical?" Devin patted him cordially on the chest.

"I don't have the blunt," Lambrook protested.

"Garring, why don't you explain to Lord Lambrook the advantages of continental travel? I have some other business I must attend to." Jeremy nodded in comprehension. Devin strode down the hall to the library with no appearance of hurry. Madeline still sat on the sofa, looking dazed.

"What happened?" he demanded.

"He needed money, so he proposed," she said with a tired sigh. "I refused him, and he threatened to tell everyone about the Incident, the duel at Elmhurst, and all of those other horrible things."

"So you tried to kill him," he prompted, seating himself beside her and crossing his legs as if preparing for a long story.

"No, I didn't mean to kill him at all. I was frightened!" she protested. I thought that he might . . . become violent."

"Hush," he said soothingly with an avuncular pat on her hand. "I know you were afraid. I don't blame you for koshing him, but it should not have come to that." He frowned sternly. "You should have come to me instantly when he proposed to blackmail you."

Madeline regarded him for a moment with weary annoyance. "I thought we were not on speaking terms."

"You should have stayed away from him. It is your fault that he had scandals to spread about. You should never—"

"My lord," Madeline interrupted calmly, "would you be so good as to go and find Mrs. Benjamin. I am certain that she is quite worried at my disappearance."

"You should be used to causing scandals by now," he replied in a clipped voice.

"Then, if you don't mind postponing my scolding. I shall go to her now." She rose unsteadily and made to exit the room.

"You will not go until I am finished," Devin proclaimed in his most autocratic voice. Madeline knew now how Frederick must feel when he got a lecture. He took her by both arms, though she showed no disposition to move away from him. "You must learn to behave with some semblance of restraint. You see now where your complete lack of regard for convention can lead you. Can you imagine how it would have looked if you had run out of the library and into the ballroom shouting about how you had killed Lord Lambrook? You are absolutely unmanageable!"

"I think you made your feelings for me clear on several other occasions," she replied coolly, with a martial gleam in her eyes. "I have seen fit not to annoy you with my attentions since then, Lord Somerton. Although I am very, very grateful that you arrived, I did not ask you to rescue me."

"You have left me alone," he agreed, though his dark brows drew together in an even fiercer manner. "I seem to be unable to leave you alone."

"Then what is it that you wish from me?" she demanded, glad that her voice hardly shook at all and clenching her hands so that he could not see their trembling.

Devin never replied. His lips descended onto hers just as he crushed her to his chest. This was definitely not the conversation he had planned, but his kiss deepened when he felt her respond. She gripped his coat and pulled him closer experiencing once more the dizzying sensation she had relived every night since the first time he'd kissed her.

Someone began pounding on the door of the

room. He sprang back from her, an expression of horror on his face. "I didn't mean to do that," he said roughly. Madeline stared at him, still panting slightly from the passion of that kiss. Her expression slowly changed to one of pain.

"Why do you keep doing it if you never want to?" she snapped. "Why do you kiss me if you dislike me?"

The pounding on the door was becoming frenzied. Devin began to look hunted, faced with this unknown intruder at the door while in the scandalous position of being locked, alone in a room with a young lady. A young lady whose temper was coming to a rapid boil.

"How can you do this to me when you know how I feel?" Madeline heard her voice become shrill. Devin appeared only to want to escape. Mrs. Benjamin nearly fell into the room once he opened the door. Her eyes widened in alarm when she saw her charge looking extremely rumpled and tearstained.

"Mrs. Benjamin," he began, with much more dignity than could be expected on such an occasion.

"You are a monster!" Madeline shouted, not caring who heard her.

"Miss Delaney, is slightly overset."

"So I see." Mrs. Benjamin regarded him with a cold eye.

"She has just done me the honor of agreeing to become my bride."

"I detest you!" Madeline cried out. She then stared, openmouthed, at Devin.

"I shall call on her father at the earliest opportunity tomorrow." He smiled with a sudden, bright ease at the shocked faces of Mrs. Benjamin and Madeline, and then exited the room pleased enough to whistle happily through the corridor and kiss the hostess on the cheek on the way out.

Madeline sat in the drawing-room window seat and stared out the window in blank misery. Dressed by Mrs. Benjamin in her finest cream-colored India muslin and with her hair pulled up into a tight, demure knot, she felt like a stupid rag doll with a pretty, painted porcelain head sticking out of a froth of laces. This humiliation was greater than any disgrace she had ever suffered. Her father, who had spent the last ten minutes smiling at her and sweating profusely, now rubbed his palms vigorously on his breeches and began bobbing his head. His smile became positively radiant.

"Well!" He stood and began to pace the room, regarding his daughter's apathy with no small degree of apprehension. "I assume that Mrs. Benjamin has instructed you on the proper . . . ahem . . . proper etiquette of the situation?"

Madeline replied in a dampening tone that she had.

"Heh! Well then! It is quite an honor, my dear,

a good deal better than we could have hoped, wouldn't you say?" He shot an anxious glance at the figure on the window seat. "A countess! Your mama would have been so very pleased."

"Would she?" she replied in a scathing tone. "Would she be pleased to know that I have entrapped a man who despises me?"

"What? Nonsense! He wouldn't have offered his hand if . . . Who could despise you?" He set down the ormolu clock that he had been examining as if he had never seen it before and gave his daughter a hard stare. "Now, I won't have you balking at this match because of some romantic notion. He has said that he would make an offer, and since it is the first offer you have had since . . . the . . . the Incident, I will not have you suddenly becoming overnice in your ideas about marriage!" Madeline slumped and turned again to the window. "He will be here soon, and after a talk with me, I shall send him in to you and you will say 'Yes, thank you.' Do you hear me?"

"Yes, Papa," Madeline replied in a colorless voice.

"You will probably find that you enjoy being a countess," he said cajolingly. "You can have parties and all of that nonsense, and his lordship told me that you will like his sisters very much." He patted her shoulder. "And," he added brightly, "he is having your cousin Frederick come to visit for the winter."

Madeline smiled faintly and turned her attention back out the window. Her father resumed his tour of the room, muttering quietly. Suddenly, Madeline stiffened and shrank back into the plum damask drapes. "He is here."

The door knocker sounded to affirm this, and Lord Delaney jumped.

"Well!" He began to smile and bob his head again. "This is a very momentous day, indeed." He started toward the door, swabbing his face with his handkerchief. "Mind me, Madeline." He turned back to her in the doorway. "I won't have you spoiling this with one of your wild schemes." He shook his finger threateningly and then shut the door behind him with a heavy hand.

When Devin entered the room a very few minutes later he found his intended in an indecorous posture with one leg swung over the window ledge. His eyebrows rose only slightly. "Good afternoon, Miss Delaney. May I help you in?" Besides a slight gurgle in her throat, she did not resist when he took her hand and assisted her to climb back into the room. "You will start a new fashion," he drawled. "All young ladies will be exiting drawing rooms through the windows for the purpose of showing off such a remarkable expanse of leg."

Madeline blushed darkly, but managed to bite back any comment.

"Quite remarkable," he said brazenly, looking her full in the face. His gray eyes were enigmati-

cally pale. She removed her hand from his in a
deliberate motion and retired to the sofa. She sat
there in silence, staring fixedly in front of her. It
became a very long silence. At last, she felt him
seat himself beside her.

"Miss Delaney, I do not know what it is that you
are scheming today, but I do not have time for
missish games." He paused, but she did not respond. "Well, Miss Delaney, I have long held you
in the highest esteem—"

Here he was interrupted by a derisive snort.

"You are determined to make this hell for me,
aren't you?" Their eyes met with mutual expressions of tense challenge.

"Miss Delaney, you have long driven me to the
brink of insanity, and I feel now compelled to ask
for your hand in marriage."

Madeline folded her hands tightly in her lap
and drew in a sharp breath. "I am not unsensi-
ble of the honor you do me, your lordship, but
please understand that I cannot accept your offer."

"Why not?" The strange tone in his voice made
her look quickly at him, but his expression was
merely impassively curious.

"Don't be stupid. You know why not. You loathe
me."

"I hardly think that that is a good basis for us
not to be married." He shrugged flippantly and
stretched out his long legs before him.

"You are only proposing to me out of a mis-
placed sense of honor, and I cannot allow that.

We were found in an . . . an awkward situation last night, but that is no reason for you to throw away your life."

"Your chivalry is praiseworthy, Miss Delaney, however, I am afraid that I must insist on our engagement."

Madeline folded her arms belligerently and set her jaw. "What about me?" she demanded. "What about my being forced to throw away *my* life?"

He did not respond for a moment, but when he did, his voice was icy. "I am afraid that you should have thought of that before."

"It was my fault that I was practically abducted by Lambrook? It was my fault that you kissed me?" She thought she felt his shoulder tighten, but she could not unsay the words.

Lord Somerton stood in one graceful motion. He turned and towered above her. "No, my dear, that was my lack of judgment. And, believe me, I am being forced to pay the price. I am beginning to think that Lambrook was the fortunate one."

"Lambrook! What happened to him?" She looked up sharply in astonishment.

Devin flushed faintly, and his lips thinned. "I am surprised to hear that you still care for him after he revealed his character last night."

"Don't be a nitwit, Devin." Madeline scowled and made an impatient gesture with her hands. "Just tell me what happened to him."

"Garring escorted him aboard the HMS *Vanity*

early this morning. He is bound for Jamaica. I am sorry that I did not consult you on the matter."

For the first time that day, Madeline laughed. "The *Vanity?* How terribly ironic! Oh, I am so glad! You are marvelous." She laughed again at the thought of Lambrook swabbing the deck in his splendid waistcoat and high shirtpoints.

"Indeed," Devin remarked, unmoved by her levity. "I shall send an announcement of our engagement to the *Times* this afternoon."

"No!" Madeline leapt to her feet. "I won't do it!"

He took her shoulders in a tight grip and looked down into her face. "I do not enjoy feeling like Lambrook. I would never force you to do something you find this distasteful if it were not entirely necessary. You have been on the brink of ostracism since the Lambrook affair began. You were closeted with him alone last night for a length of time and then were seen . . . embracing me. If you wish to remain accepted, even by the fringes of society, you will have to marry either Lambrook or myself. I regret that by my unpropitious action last night, I have whittled your choice down to one"—he gave her a grim half-smile—"unless you fancy Jamaica."

There was a long silence while Madeline stared at him, overcome by his close presence. She inhaled the scent of his soap and steadied herself. "I will consider your offer of marriage," she said at last.

"I take that as acceptance," he replied tersely

and dropped his hands from her arms. He turned and did not appear to notice that Madeline dropped onto the sofa and burst into tears as he left the room.

Sixteen

"I simply do not understand why you are kicking up such dust over this." Mrs. Benjamin shook her head as she gathered up a breakfast tray that Madeline had not touched. Madeline only moaned dramatically and burrowed further under the covers.

The older woman set down the tray with slightly more violence than was due to the Sevres china and seated herself with a harrumph. Madeline did not respond. "Dearest, you know your father would never force you to marry anyone you did not have a tolerable . . . fondness for. However, I think you are being a good deal too romantic in your notions about marriage. Love is a fine thing to read about in a novel, pet, but it was never meant to be applied to life. You have always known that you would be obliged to make a match with someone suitable, and I simply cannot see how you could do better than Mr. Forth, Lord Somerton—whoever he is now. Especially after . . . Well, you certainly looked as though you were fond of him! You are fortunate that I did not mention the circumstances of Forth's offer to your father. The shock would have killed him, I'm sure." She gave Madeline a sharp look.

"You don't understand, Benny. The man despises me."

"He didn't look as though he was despising you the other night," her duenna replied with some asperity.

"Well, he does." Madeline sat up in bed, her head a mass of curlpapers.

"He wouldn't have proposed if he did," Mrs. Benjamin countered.

"I will not marry him!"

"Why not?"

"Because I love him."

Mrs. Benjamin regarded her charge for a long moment. "That is a very odd reason for not wanting to marry someone," she said at last. "Particularly when he has already proposed."

"Benny! How could I possibly marry someone who does not love me? When I have forced him into offering for me?"

"Good heavens, girl! First you tell me you hate him, then you plot and plan to find a way to make him marry you, and now you announce that you will not marry him even though he has asked for your hand. I never met a more difficult creature. You have been entirely too much indulged as a child. You should have had a brother who boxed your ears on occasion."

She watched Madeline scowl for a moment and then sighed. "Stop making this out to be a

Cheltemham tragedy. You will make him a fine wife. I would advise you to forget all of this nonsense and get up. You know he has sent over word that he would like to take you riding in the park this afternoon." Mrs. Benjamin rose from the chair and brushed her hands together to signal that the discussion was at an end.

Madeline threw back the covers and leapt out of bed. With shaking hands, she began to tear out the curlpapers and brush her hair. "Do send up some hot water, Benny. What's here has gone quite cold."

Her companion watched her frenzied activity for a moment and then smiled with a look of satisfaction that would have infuriated Madeline if she had seen it. "I will send Letty up to help you get ready," she murmured deferentially.

She would not have felt quite so complacent if she had known that Madeline was racketing her brains to formulate a plan.

Madeline watched in satisfaction as Devin's expression changed to one of horror when he looked up and saw her descending the stairs. It had been a triumph of subterfuge to slip out wearing the horrific ensemble without Mrs. Benjamin's positive veto. The long-suffering Letty had had to be threatened with dismissal, and even then, she hovered near the head of the stairs, twisting her apron.

The dress Madeline had insisted upon was ac-

tually an evening gown and not at all suited for a
ride in the park. It was cut far too deeply in the
neckline for daytime wear, and a shocking expanse of bosom and arm was displayed. The scarf
she dragged behind her was a striking chartreuse
that clashed madly with the rosy pink of the gown.
The emerald kid gloves were a masterpiece of Ital-
ian workmanship with their van dyked points of
lemon yellow. Her shoes were blue. Looking Devin
directly in the eyes, she reached up to her head
and pulled out a pin. A large chunk of her hair
came tumbling from the side of her upswept coif.

"Are you quite ready?" he asked, fully recovered.

"Oh, yes, I am ready at last. I am so sorry to
keep you waiting this three-quarters of an hour,
but I just can't ever seem to be on time." She
laughed loudly and clapped on a high-crowned
bonnet trimmed with large clusters of grapes and
crimson ribbons that looked as though they had
been hastily added. She swept out of the house,
trying to ignore Metworth's surprised cough.

Devin regarded her intently for a moment and
then handed her into his phaeton, apparently
oblivious to Madeline's incessant flow of chatter.
"You are looking well," he commented mildly at
last.

"Why, thank you my lord! I am so relieved to
be released from the strictures of debutante dress.
Why, when I am a married woman, I shall be able
to dress in any way I like! I shall need a great deal
of new clothes because I intend to rig myself out

in just the kind of style I really like." She shot him an assessing look from under the bonnet.

"Naturally."

"It shall be ferociously expensive, I imagine."

"Fortunately, several of my estates are unentailed," he returned with an easy smile.

"And I should like to live in London all of the time," she announced loudly. "I would be perfectly happy to never go to the country again. And I think I would like to throw parties every week. Oh, dear, that could be a bit expensive, too. Plus I have no notion of how to run a house. It could become a bit difficult with all the servants. I simply cannot seem to even manage to plan the menu for dinner." She laughed again and added a snort for good measure.

"I think I will redecorate whatever house we buy in the height of Egyptian style. I simply adore crocodiles. The rooms will be perfectly loaded with gilt crocodiles. And palm trees." She looked about her and then stood up in the open carriage and began waving and shouting wildly. "I thought I saw someone I knew," she explained, when this elicited no response other than a slightly repressed smile. She seated herself again.

"You really could not think of any better plan to turn me off?" Devin asked quietly as he turned into the park.

"I am prone to fits, you know."

"You shall not make me release you from this engagement, Madeline."

"I have been accused by some of being quite mad."

"I do not disagree." He smiled at her in an infuriatingly placid manner and continued to drive around the park, acknowledging cheerfully the bows of his acquaintances."

"If you do not take me home this instant, I shall—I shall sing," she announced belligerently.

"How lovely. I do hope it is something melodramatic. Do you know all of the verses? The park is quite crowded, and it could take some time for us to make our way around." His gray eyes had something of a martial light to them.

"I shall sing very loudly," she warned, clearing her throat.

"Do try to stay on key," Devin said, in a peculiar tone. "I should hate for you to disappoint Lady Champhill."

Madeline started and saw that he was quite right. Lady Champhill had seen them and had turned to guide her horse toward the phaeton, a triumphant expression on her face.

"Miss Delaney! Lord Somerton!" she cried out in ringing tones of utmost delight. "I have heard the astounding news! You are engaged! What a surprise that was to all of us, I assure you." She smiled very brightly. "You are sly, Miss Delaney. None of us had any idea you knew his lordship so well as to attach his interest. So entirely sudden it was!" She sidled her dashing roan gelding closer to Madeline's side of the phaeton.

It flung up its head and rolled its eyes in a way

that seemed particularly bad-tempered. Madeline eyed the spirited beast and its rider with equal distaste. Lady Champhill was looking annoyingly beautiful in a deep blue riding habit with military-style frogging down its front.

Arabella flung an arch smile at Somerton. "But Miss Delaney has always had so *many* beaux." She suddenly opened her eyes wide. "Did you hear that Lambrook has disappeared? It is quite mysterious. Quite scandalous, really." She gave Madeline a honeyed expression of sympathy. "Perhaps he was brokenhearted." She laughed. "Oh, don't be cross with me, my dear Miss Delaney. I declare, the look you just gave me was practically murderous! It is tragically unfair, when I am the one who is to be pitied. Devin, I mean Lord Somerton, was engaged to take me out riding yesterday, and he entirely abandoned me."

Madeline looked to Devin. "I regret that I was unable to take you out, Arabella, I hope you got the note I sent around to you explaining that I would be unavailable," he replied.

"I was *devastated* nonetheless. I see now that you were busy being 'unavailable' with Miss Delaney." She laughed again. "How delighted your father must be, Miss Delaney. He must have been so relieved that you are at last engaged. I mean, he must have had a terrible time turning down the *multitude* of offers you have no doubt received!"

"I hope that you will pardon us, Arabella, but I see an acquaintance is trying to attract our attention. I hope I may someday be forgiven for the offense of having had to cancel our appointment."

"Of course you are forgiven, you ridiculous man! You may make it up to me anytime you like." She smiled meaningfully at Somerton and moved her horse to allow them to pass on. "And, Miss Delaney," she called out after them, "I cannot tell you how much I *adore* that dress!"

Madeline clenched her teeth and refused to allow herself to tug her bodice higher over her cleavage. Devin turned the phaeton off the main road, and they drove down the smaller, quiet path in silence. Madeline sat looking stonily ahead until she noticed that Somerton's shoulders were shaking with repressed laughter.

She turned on him in fury. "How dare you laugh at me?"

"I am sorry; I cannot help it," he replied, turning his laugh into a cough behind his hand.

"Nothing delights you more than to humiliate me, does it?"

"I have not humiliated you. You have done it to yourself." He looked at her with a peculiar expression that was almost fond and nearly helpless.

"You would much rather have married Lady Champhill. I spoiled everything for you." She scowled.

"I never had the least intention of marrying that vulgar woman." He glanced at her out of the corner of his eye. "Especially when I have the opportunity to marry a woman so much more vulgar."

"Do shut up, you horrid man."

Abruptly, he stopped the horses and flung the reins to the groom. "Walk for a while with me, Miss Delaney," he said, leaping to the ground and offering his hand to help her down. "We shall quarrel in private."

She threw him a look of disgust, but put her gloved hand in his. She cringed at the garish clash of colors on her arm. He was right; she had humiliated herself. She should have known that annoying him with tasteless dress and obnoxious behavior would hardly be enough to break their betrothal.

"You do look like some kind of very exotic bird," he said, noting the direction of her glance. "Perhaps you will start a new fashion. We shall set you up as a kind of anti-Beau Brummell." His mouth quirked ever so slightly on the left side, but the rest of his face remained impassive.

"You are infuriating," she announced, jerking her hand from his as soon as she was able and beginning to walk with long, unladylike strides. Devin easily kept up with her, but did not offer her his arm.

"And so are you," he replied amiably.

"I should have gone with my first plan."

"Leaping from the drawing-room window?" His gray eyes twinkled briefly, but were quickly veiled by dark lashes.

"That was not a plan; that was a reaction," she retorted tartly. "My first plan was to leave a note saying that I was eloping to Gretna Green."

"With . . . ?" he raised his brows questioningly.

"Oh, I don't know, some suitor or other. You needn't be nasty by reminding me that I don't have so many these days. I was going to invent one." She sighed and absently curled the haphazard lock of unpinned hair around her finger. "But that plan posed some problems."

"I should think that traveling alone to Gretna Green with an imaginary suitor would." He smiled, and they walked on in silence for a moment. "For instance, who would have paid for the license?

"Yes, yes. Ha-ha. It was a stupid idea from the start." She shot him a rueful look. "Besides, Lord Cleverness, you don't need a license to be married at Gretna Green. A blacksmith would have done me just fine."

"I think that you deserve better than to be married to an imaginary suitor by a blacksmith at Gretna Green. Elopements to Scotland are so trite . . . so overdone." He rubbed his chin with his long fingers. "Perhaps you could have eloped with the blacksmith and caught a packet to Australia. That would have been dramatic."

She could not help but laugh even though she felt miserable.

"But you could not go through with the elopement," Devin prompted her, when she did not respond further.

"No."

"Why not?"

"I . . . I don't know." She swallowed hard and looked away.

He stopped and took her arm. "Is the idea of marrying me so very distasteful, Madeline?" he asked quietly.

"No"—she looked resolutely at the ground and forced her voice to be steady—"but the idea of forcing you into marriage is."

"Perhaps you have forgotten the circumstances that precipitated our betrothal."

His hands upon her shoulders were warm, and she could feel her pulse throb heavily in her throat at his touch. She raised her eyes to his for a moment, but, with a little, strangled intake of breath, instantly dropped them again to his cravat.

"No," she managed at last.

"I was kissing you."

"I recall." Their voices had dropped almost to whispers.

"And, my dear"—he spoke close to her ear—"it was not because of some wild scheme of yours."

"No?" she raised her eyes to his, and he caught her face in his hands. His kiss was tender only for a moment before she pressed her body to his and silently demanded more from him.

"I have loved you from the start," he said at last with a breathless laugh. "From the day we met on the street in front of Watier's."

"What?!" she exclaimed in horror, "Oh, don't love me from then! Love me from—"

"From when I knew that you had connived to have Lambrook locked out of his room?"

"Oh, dear, not then either. I behaved so badly!" She lodged herself more firmly into his arms and twisted her arms around his neck. "Perhaps . . ." She paused and thought dreamily for a moment.

"From the day you acted like Lady Champhill at the Royal Gallery?" he laughed softly.

"Heavens no! Maybe from"—she smiled up at him, her blue eyes mischievous—"from now on?"

"As you wish, my love. From now on."

Put a Little Romance in Your Life With
Janelle Taylor

Put a Little Romance in Your Life With
Fern Michaels

__Dear Emily	0-8217-5676-1	$6.99US/$8.50CAN
__Sara's Song	0-8217-5856-X	$6.99US/$8.50CAN
__Wish List	0-8217-5228-6	$6.99US/$7.99CAN
__Vegas Rich	0-8217-5594-3	$6.99US/$8.50CAN
__Vegas Heat	0-8217-5758-X	$6.99US/$8.50CAN
__Vegas Sunrise	1-55817-5983-3	$6.99US/$8.50CAN
__Whitefire	0-8217-5638-9	$6.99US/$8.50CAN

Call toll free **1-888-345-BOOK** to order by phone or use this coupon to order by mail.
Name_____
Address_____
City _____ State _____Zip_____
Please send me the books I have checked above.
I am enclosing $_____
Plus postage and handling* $_____
Sales tax (in New York and Tennessee) $_____
Total amount enclosed $_____
*Add $2.50 for the first book and $.50 for each additional book.
Send check or money order (no cash or CODs) to:
Kensington Publishing Corp., 850 Third Avenue, New York, NY 10022
Prices and Numbers subject to change without notice.
All orders subject to availability.
Check out our website at **www.kensingtonbooks.com**

More Zebra Regency Romances

Celebrate Romance With Two of Today's Hottest Authors

Meagan McKinney

Meryl Sawyer